THE FIRST BOOK OF NERO AND SPORUS

DELICATUS

S.P. SOMTOW

DIPLODOCUS PRESS · 2023

This novel first appeared as the first 31 chapters of a serial in Amazon Vella in 2022.

ISBN:
Kindle Edition: none
paperback: 978-1940999-82-1
hardcover: 978-1940999-83-8

0 9 8 7 6 5 4 3 2 1
First Edition

I started writing this novel
because in so many ways
it's the story of my adopted son Mikey
he too went from a homeless orphan
to hobnobbing with royals and myth makers
he too changed his gender
almost as frequently as his clothes
he too had visions and dreams
of gods and demons
and he too was destroyed by them

No one your life touched
will ever forget you.

DELICATUS

Sol omnibus lucet
The sun shines on everybody

— Petronius

I

GODDESS

… chains and the sea …

Hold still. The rouge has to be even.

It seems I will end as I began, my feet chained to a wall, and a roar in my ears. Though then it was the ocean, and now it is a crowd. Both hungry, both eager to swallow up souls.

Don't talk so much. Wait. Let me finish your lips first.

My life begins with the wooden wall and the roaring sea. To remember further back is to be in hell, and so I won't. Though snatches of it have haunted me all along. Burning villages. Blood. A crucifixion at a crossroads, an auction in an agora.

Smudged!

Don't be all nervous. You have time to finish this. And I … I feel like talking. You must let me. There are things I wish I could tell someone. Especially now, when I'm about to enter the next plane of my existence.

I've been a refugee. I've been a slave boy. I've been an empress. I've mated with two gods, and soon I'll be a god myself. And all before my twentieth birthday.

Again! Should I mix the rouge myself? Hold still.

Does it matter?

We all know how this will end.

Demeter's daughter, spirit of spring, Proserpina the fair, comes forth among the flowers, trees and meadows. The earth opens up, and from the gates of Hades itself emerges Pluto, Lord of the Dead, with his three-headed hound in tow. Violently he seizes the maiden, drags her onto his chariot, kicking and screaming, quirting his skeletal horses down into the bowels of the earth as the flowers begin to wilt, as the fruit falls and rots on the barren ground, as the leaves turn brittle and yellow, as cold envelops the world.

You know how Ceres-Demeter searches the desolate world. How the plants mourn, how the soil turns to stone and can no longer sustain life, how men and animals begin to starve for lack of sustenance. You know Proserpina's mother descends to the depths of hell where her daughter is now queen. How she pleads with the dark god until he relents. How Proserpina is tricked into eating six seeds of a pomegranate … and so must live six months of the year in the dark realm of the dead. How the earth blooms again when she returns, how the earth dies she when returns to the cold.

I shall act out that drama. With all the violence that entails.

Such is the command of Himself the Divine Vitellius, my Emperor and my God. This, he has told me, shall be how I atone for my infamy. Not that I ever *chose* infamy. It chose me.

If you are going to be of ignoble birth, don't be beautiful. You will come to a bad end. As I already have. The Rape of Proserpina is merely the garnish.

This being the Roman *ludi*, of course, Proserpina doesn't

come back. No one comes back from such an outing. Oh, perhaps the odd gladiator, if the mob loves him, if he sticks it out long enough to earn the wooden sword. People like me, we are not the main course.   We're but a kind of amuse-bouche in between the serious fights, and we don't get to ask for a thumbs-up.

Doubtless, the "actor" chosen to play Pluto will be some priapic monstrosity selected for sole purpose of leaving me as ripped and bloody as possible before the chariot drags me round and round and the crowds cheer each bump, each jolt. Doubtless some savage from Germania or Nubia.

No point in imagining every second of your agony in advance, Divinity. You'll have plenty of time to enjoy it in the flesh, if you see what I mean.

Impudent slave!

Look who's talking!

I know. I am one to talk. I was once lowlier than you, and soon shall be again. So let me talk. In a few hours, my voice will be stilled forever.   And you, junior assistant cosmetic artist of the imperial household, sent to make me beautiful for the last time by the Grace of none other than Himself the Divine Vitellius, third emperor in this year of many emperors but perhaps not the last ... you will go back to painting the faces of the mighty, being slapped around from time to time, and dying like a shriveled old dog on the master's country estate.

You called me *Divinity* just now, not just in deference to the role I will play today, but because I have been a God. And I have mated with a God. Or Gods. And let me tell you, the Gods are no better in bed than ordinary men.

Lift up the mirror.

I want my eyelids gold ... real gold dust, bound with the

boiled bones of horses. It doesn't matter if it blocks my pores. It will not be for long.

And the kohl-rimmed eyes … they must be black. My eyelashes *will* be seen even by the plebeians!

Oh, such a decrepit stage for my final performance. Big, the Circus Maximus, but strangely déclassé. They have everything here from chariot races to executions, gladiators to Greek theater. One day some Emperor will build a proper venue. Not this dusty space that hasn't been repaired in a century or two. When I was Empress I sometimes told Lucius, the one you call Nero, he should peel off some of the domestic budget he set aside for his Golden House to build a proper amphitheater for games. Doesn't look like I will live to see such a colosseum. It would be nice to die in a venue worthy of my godhead.

Hold still!

I *am* holding still. I mean, you do have me chained up.

Chained up, just like the day I first came to Rome.

… chains and the sea…

Still, Divinity!

… chains and the sea…

This place is rooted to the ground, but it reminds me of that ship. Me, chained in the hold with a few dozen others. Scrawny. The roar of the sea, the roar of the crowd … the bite of the chains on my thin skin … here the walls are moist with sweat and tears … there they were damp from the brine of the sea. The smell of the ocean, the sweaty smell of human misery … it is the same. This cell of stone, that cell of wood … the twin imprisonments of my life's journey.

I'm going to talk … I'm going to tell all of it. To pass the time before they call me out. Someone should know about my life. In times to come, *someone* must surely speak of Sporus, my journey from slave boy, fellator of senators, to Empress of Rome, to Goddess of Spring, to Queen of the Dead.

II

PIRATE

... a village? ... You ask if I recall ... a village?

Before the chains and the sea, no clear memories. No memories at all.

In dreams, I can see a sun-drenched village. A clear blue sky. A woman in the woods, me tugging at the edge of her tunic. Her eyes ... clear, green, her face furrowed, lined.

The woods in the foothills, village in the plain.

Smoke tendrilling up from thatched huts.

Savoring the stillness.

Now and then, the song of a thrush. We are picking mushrooms. I look at my mother and ... I don't know ... her eyes ... I remember. I remember the eyes. The warmth.

... or was it a palace?

Am I in the bath, being oiled, feet dangling in the tepidarium, my mother idly sipping a goblet of Lesbian wine from a painted kylix? I see the winecup so clearly but am I remembering from somewhere else, from the home of the sybaritic Gaius Petronius?

Is the song a slave girl from Nubia, singing some nonsense from her native land, from the atrium as she cleans? Am I prince or peasant?

Only my mother's eyes are the same.

My mother's eyes … and the screaming.

At first I think it's a lot of thrushes. It's high-pitched and thick and faint, a distant wall of keening. It takes a while to realize the entire village is screaming. And burning. They're not thrushes but the dying, each pinprick shriek a sound-smear in the clear bright sky.

They're coming through the forest, clanging their shields and banging on trees like hunters driving out game. I don't see faces, only soulless eyes. They catch me. They catch my mother. They swing her, brain her against a tree-trunk, and the sound of smashing skull on hardwood is indelibly seared in my memory —

Or is it? Are the dead-eyed savages striding through the atrium, spearing the men and lassoing the women — and is it the brick wall where my mother's brains are smeared? — Oh, I am confused — I have lost my past. Oh, I have invented so many pasts for myself, they all have merged into a confused tapestry — but all these pasts converge in a single place —

A line of pathetic creatures, barely human, shackled, being urged on by the ones with the dead eyes. Single file. The ones too sick to walk, they urge on with blows, or just let them go limp and be dragged along by those still clinging to life. And the line goes on and on, and me with them, and I don't even know who I have been chained to. I just know that we walk and walk, and after some days it is all downhill so we slip and slide and knock our shins on sharp stones and slither in mud, and we walk through a nightmare landscape, past burning villages, dead bodies putrefying, and then we are shoved, still chained but now only by twos or fours, onto rickety boats, and thence onto a ship.

A *ship!*

I have never seen a ship. I've never seen the sea, let alone *smelled* the sea.

There's awe. There's pain, overwhelming pain, not just from the blows, not just from the lashing, but hunger, thirst, and heartache. The wind of the waves and the dry heaves because you want to vomit but there is nothing to throw up.

Being completely ignored. No one to answer questions. To ask is to be beaten. I haven't even heard my own language yet. I don't know where I am going. We are jammed in the hold. It's chaos.

The ship begins to move. We can barely see in the hold. There's one smoky lamp. I do not know if it is day or night. I listen to murmurings. I think that we are slaves.

Only a few days have gone by but I'm already not sure where it is I came from. I've walled off the past. It's how my mind is, I think. I build compartments, and I throw away the key. You'll see … it's how I will survive through lightning transformations. I am like some kind of insect. I suffer unspeakable pain and I emerge as someone completely different … not even the same species, any more than a caterpillar is a butterfly.

Later, I will read about transformations in an old book by Publius Ovidius Naso, in a language which in that moment

I have yet to learn. He says, *Omnia mutantur, nihil interit.* He means something like "Everything changes ... yet nothing perishes." But he is wrong. Because you can't change back. Everything is *always* perishing. Your soul, your identity isn't some unchanging shard of light within that is never affected by the outside world.

And that very first afternoon on the ship, my first metamorphosis begins in earnest. The dead-eyed people took off my chains. A woman came to me and led me by the hand, up rickety steps into the sunlight. She made me remove every remaining rag that still clung to me, glued by blood and sweat and dried mucus.

Carefully, she washed me, combed my hair, scrubbed me with olive oil, and scraped the oil away with a strigil. "There you are," she said at last. She had a kind of tenderness. I could understand her, though she formed her words differently from what I was used to.

I said, "Are you my new mother?"

She laughed and said words in a foreign language. Then she said, laughing, "Mother! I'm a pirate."

She held up a polished plate of brass and I saw myself. I had never seen myself before, did not know who stared back up at me. The boy in the mirror was scrawny, pale, with straggly, blond hair.

I had big eyes.

"The eyes," she said. "The eyes do the selling." She brushed on a little kohl. "Try to smile."

I managed a wan smile.

"You'll do."

They left me like that. Naked, oiled, and lightly brushed with perfume. My eyes were brightened with a little kohl.

I was not chained, but there was nowhere to go. I watched the open sea. In the distance, big fishes leaped. I allowed myself a moment of pleasure.

"They are not fish," said a voice. "A pod of dolphins."

Startled, I turned. I saw a man in a kind of armor — assembled from bits and pieces. One eye was dead and hard, like all the other captors on this ship. The other eye was missing.

"You can stare," he said.

He came closer, put a callused hand on my shoulder. "I need to study the dolphins. Usually they are our friends, but sometimes they mean danger. They speak, in their own way."

He bends to look at my face. He turns my face this way and that.

I am passive. I am shaking.

"You're a good one," he said. "Where are you from?"

"You speak like me."

"One of many languages. But you will learn another soon. Two, if you fetch the right price."

"Am I for sale?"

"The world is for sale, child, and you are owned without even knowing it."

"And who are the owners?"

"Only the gods. They're all completely uninterested in the human race, sitting in their sky palaces. None of them will do anything. They will leave the world to fester in its own shit. Only one god lives in the real world. And he's the most troublesome one of all."

I did not understand any of that.

"You are a prime piece of merchandise," he says. "But the useful life of a delicatus is brief. You'll flower for a day, and then — poof — you will be too old. Learn to read and write. Be useful. Or they'll sell you to some filthy lupanar when they're done with you."

"What is a delicatus?" I said.

He shook his head. "I suppose I will have to break you in," he said, and there was a twinge of sadness in his voice, regret, almost. Then he took me into a private cabin, and subjected me to the most painful, most humiliating, most soul-destroying acts, beyond anything I imagined possible. In that hour, he broke me, and I searched my mind in vain for any trace of anyone I had ever been.

I sat on the floor, bleeding, weeping, and he said softly, "Save your tears. You still own your tears. Do not give them away."

"After what you did —!" I said, crying even more disconsolately.

"That was just business, boy," he said. "I meant no harm. And you will see by tomorrow, there is no permanent damage; I owe that much to the client. But now that I've shattered your identity, let's give you a new one. Did you come from a village, an innocent flower of the field? Were you actually a prince, scion of some barbarous nation?"

"I don't know."

"Find a good past. A colorful past can really up the bidding," he said. "Prince, I think."

I dried my eyes with my arm.

"And we must give you a name."

"I *have* a name!"

But in that moment, I could not recollect it.

"Ah, ah, you must have a name."

"You haven't told me yours," I said. Although he had used me like a rag.

"You do not need my name," he said. "It would only be another burdensome memento of a past you should forget. You, however … your fate could be to serve in a great house … and to be cast away. Or it could be to serve and worm your way upwards, learn skills, become a freedman, even own an entire stable of delicati. You are a seedling — and I hope you will not be cast on stony ground."

He peered at me with his one eye. "A seedling! You will be called *Sporos*. That is Greek, a civilized language; the Romans will undoubtedly coarsen it to Sporus."

My captor pulled me up and pushed me out onto the deck. I was still naked, still bleeding a little.

The sun's beginning to set. The wind is cool. Dolphins are leaping, more agitated now.

"Are they telling us something?" I asked him.

One-eye leaned over the edge and stared into the distance, where the dolphins breached against the face of the sun. When he turns back his eye seems bloodshot. "Romani!" he shouts. "Outrun them!"

I hear it now. Faint but regular. Oars slapping on the water. The thud of a drum. Hundreds of oars maybe.

And I see the ships. Three of them. Bearing down on us. Swiftly.

Cacophony broke loose around me. Another drumbeat from below deck, frantic. Oars too, but on this ship they hit the water almost randomly, not synchronized. The drum accelerated. We were moving away from the Romans.

"Lock up the slaves!" someone screamed. Someone was bolting down the entrance to the hold. In the confusion no one saw me, a naked, helpless boy, cowering. I could hear the captives shrieking, bewildered, in the dark, from below. Pirates were readying weapons. The drumming reached fever pitch.

But we were getting away, weren't we? The Romans would not catch up. I would be sold. There was no escape. One-eye stalked about, barking orders.

Then I turned toward the prow and saw that another ship was almost on top of us. We were about to be rammed. I could see the corvus being lowered. I heard the crash as the corvus landed. I heard screaming. I heard trampling, disciplined, relentless. Fire-arrows were raining down now. The Romans' boots banging, a terrifying, steady rhythm. I saw the one-eyed pirate brandishing a sword, roaring.

So you were rescued! How exciting! The Roman army plucked you from the mouth of hell! I do love an adventure, but you must hold still. We want to make sure your audience sees you. Even the ones in the uppermost tiers, the women, the slaves. Now, tell me more about the rescue.

Was that a rescue?

Or was it something worse?

III

CRUCIFIXION

… chains and the sea …

Hold still. The rouge has to be even.

How much longer?

A while. There is a mass crucifixion going on.

Oh, who?

Some cult that forbids worshipping the Emperor.

It serves them right, then. How boring. I've seen so many. But you never forget your first, do you. When criminals are crucified en masse in the arena, it is entertainment of course. The display crosses let people in the stands get a better view of the faces.

But when it's not a show, it's often quite banal. Except, perhaps, to the crucified.

In what people are already calling the "good old days", they dipped them in pitch as well, and set them ablaze, and they burned through the night like human torches … though the screams did not last long.

The good old days, really, don't we all agree! A singing emperor and a burning city. Legend! And to think that you — you — were debauched by a God!

You forget … I am going to *be* a God soon.
You are. So hold still. The eyes must be perfect.

The Romans escorted the pirate vessel close to shore. We were sorted into pirates and cargo. Cargo was catalogued from most valuable to least: first came statues, works of art, jewelry, last mundanities like amphoras of olive oil; we were worth less than the art, but was that surprising? Human life is brief — art is eternal.

The pirates were shackled. We were chained. No one had thought to find me any clothes, but I was wearing a lot of dirt and blood — other people's, I am sure. There were other people with no clothes. Slaves don't really need clothes. I was chained next to the woman who had made me beautiful — beautiful enough to be savagely violated. She did not look at me. I wondered whether she knew what had happened to me … how much she had known beforehand. We squatted on the sand. The pirates did not squat. They were chained with their arms between poles, and were made to stand; when one looked like he was going to fall over, he got a whack of the flagellum, and stayed standing.

Where we landed, the beach was just a strip; beyond, on higher ground, were grassy areas alternating with boulders. The sky was a brilliant blue. Later I will think of this place as Greece, but really it could have been another part of the empire.

A man walked up and down the rows of merchandise. Next to him, a wizened little man was making notes on a wax tablet. The man's armor was polished, his plumes bright red; he did not look at all like someone who had just been in a sea-battle. He moved, in a leisurely way, from object to object, murmuring to the scribe, who said repeatedly, *"Ita, Centurio, ita, centurio,"* nodding as he scribbled. I had heard the word *centurio* before. He was a centurion, a commander of a hundred men.

They were getting nearer. He spoke to one captive, then another. I said, "Sir, are we being rescued?"

He clapped his hands and had my chains struck off. I had not expected to be understood but he spoke to me in my own language. "It depends on what you mean by rescue," he said.

He put his hand on my shoulder. He motioned and someone brought me a tunica. It was torn, but I'd never felt such soft fabric against my skin.

"How do you know my language?" I asked him.

"On the campaigns," he said. "Come, you pretty little thing. You already have that sadness that people like you always have, the sadness hiding behind every smile. Did one of these pirates hurt you?"

I nodded.

"Come, point him out."

He led me to the pirates and I soon pointed out the leader. The single eye was not so dead now. I saw — no, *smelled* — his terror. The Centurion beckoned with his finger and two soldiers pulled him out. They began dragging him up the slope, to a patch of elevated ground.

"Come with me," the Centurion said to me.

On the incline, soldiers were cutting up tree trunks, making crude crosses. This wasn't the fine workmanship you see in the arena, perfectly straight pieces of wood teased and scraped into the right shape. These were just tree trunks, slightly trimmed, no finishing. And not the display crosses that you can see in Rome, either. The criminals'oldiers threw the one who had hurt me on the ground and started tying his arms to one of the crosses.

"Did he hurt you very much?" said the Centurion.

I nodded again.

"Right then." My captor was strangely compliant; I expected him to struggle, but was calm, almost like a sacrificial animal. The Centurion knelt down and I knelt with him. A soldier produced a monster of a nail, placed it spike down against the man's wrist. Then he gave me his hammer. I hefted it.

"Go on," said the Centurion. "You're with the grownups now. Aim well and drive the nail home."

I swung. The pain must have been unimaginable. The pirate tensed, jerked; blood spurted; but he did not cry out at all. I suppose he did not want to give me the satisfaction. I swung again and I think he fainted.

"Good lad," the Centurion said. He held me as his underlings finished the job and did the other wrist, and the feet as well. The sound the bone made, cracking … you never forget something like that.

The Centurion lifted me up and made me watch as they hoisted the pirate into an upright position. The one who had quoted Ovid to me looked at me dully. His eyes were empty. If his body was not dead already, his soul was no longer inside him.

I vomited, all over the nearly new tunica. "It's all right, lad. No one has the stomach for it at first." He wiped me off. "Did you get any satisfaction?"

I closed my eyes, remembering. "I don't think so."

I looked around and saw that it was a kind of routine process, tying, hoisting, tying, hoisting. There was a lot of screaming. Presently it was like a little grove of dying men, groaning, wheezing. Their screams gradually becoming dull. A few scavenger birds were beginning to gather.

"We don't usually use nails normally," the Centurion said. "That was a little treat, just for you. It's a mercy, really; he'll bleed out a lot quicker than these others."

The crucifixions had been done in a very orderly way, the crosses planted at regular intervals, and the soldiers showed little emotion; it was just a job.

And then they fed us.

Bread, olives, diluted wine.

We had had almost nothing for days. We sat on the beach and looked up at the forest of the dying, savoring our bread.

The Centurion was kind. He called me to his side and sat me by a fire. He didn't speak to me for a while, but instead to some companions, discussing the coming voyage, supply logistics, things I did not understand. He looked at my meager portion of bread and gave me a small piece of dried meat. Then, incredibly, an apple.

Looking around the makeshift encampment, I saw that many of the soldiers had a boy as a companion. They would bring their masters food. When their master reached out, a cup of wine would be ready without their even asking. The boys were silent shadows. I could see myself in a role like that. I didn't think I would mind him touching me.

I would have liked to know how he had learned my language "on campaign" — who he had fought, what action he had seen. Was he a Roman at all or had he once been what I was? Something, I sensed, had damaged him.

That is why he felt empathy for me. We had this in common, though my wounds were fresher. My past had been pushed behind a wall. In my present, he was the first person I felt close to. I asked him what his name was. I didn't tell him my own name, nor could I bring myself to tell him the name the pirate had given me.

He said, "You can call me Marcus, I suppose."

"Will I live with you now? Will I go on campaign with you? Will I learn languages?"

He laughed. "I am not your owner."

"But I would go of my own free will," I said.

"Lad … you don't have any free will. You're destined for my betters, I'm afraid."

"But … didn't you come to punish the pirates, to rescue us?"

"Yes … the cargo has been rescued," he said. "The state has confiscated it and it will all be auctioned off properly, not in some sordid contraband market."

"We are not to be freed?"

"Where would you go? You are a pretty thing and you will adorn some noble house — not some whorehouse in the suburra. You could accumulate a decent peculium, and once you lose your looks there's no reason you shouldn't be able to buy your freedom."

"But you unchained me! You treated me almost like … a son. Marcus, let me stay with you!"

He looked away. "A centurion may not marry," he said, "and the term of service is at least twenty-five years. A boy is better suited than a wife for these rough campaigns, and a slave is more practical; the prohibition on marriage keeps us wedded to the legion."

"Can't you buy me?"

"On nine hundred sesterces a year? You're worth ten times that at least. I hardly dare put my hand on your shoulder for fear of bruising your skin."

"Don't you love me?"

"So young, already so good at the game! Love is for the gods," he said. "We're only people. What we have is duty, desire, and hope. And if I gave you hope, I am sorry. I didn't mean to. You just reminded me of … something. Someone."

"The pirate said that there is also a human who is a god."

And Marcus fished a coin from a pouch. It was large, polished brass. I saw a portrait of a comely, slightly pudgy man. Marcus held it up to the flickering firelight. He handed it to me and I gazed at the portrait, the first time I ever saw the face of Nero Claudius Caesar Augustus Germanicus.

"Keep it," he said. "Let's call it my contribution to your peculium. A fragment of your future freedom."

Your Emperor. Your God. And for a time —
My husband.
The first, alas, of many.
And the reason I've been chosen for today's apotheosis … a mythic drama that will be acted out before the gaze of twenty thousand hungry pairs of eyes … the reason I've been chosen to play the Queen of Hell. No figure is more tragic than an empress fallen from her throne. Oh, Divinity! What times we had!
But you could not have known any of that at the time.
No. All I knew was that Marcus had me chained up again, and we were loaded back into the hold of a ship

bound for Ostia. I did not see him again on that voyage.

I think that for an afternoon I was in love. That would never happen again. I had learned my lesson.

IV

WAREHOUSE

They laughed when I gawked at Ostia.

"Whatever barbarous hamlet you came from," said the little Greek accountant, who was watching over us as we were offloaded, "compared with Ostia, is as Ostia compared to Rome."

Ostia is a port. A town with walls! There are streets lined with shophouses, crammed with people, and merchandise moving all day and all night (in Rome the carts only come out at night). The sounds! Grinding carts. Dirty water being sloshed into the streets. Music of pipes and drums. Cries of merchants. The trudging of soldiers' caligae.

The people! People of hues I had never imagined. People in outlandish costumes. Now I can identify them, then they were a blur, the smells of delicious food and shit mingling in the streets as they marched us to the warehouse district; for we were merchandise, not to be housed with the people.

It was a room with high, barred windows that seemed to be at street level; we must be underground. Our chains were generous in length, allowing us to move about quite a bit, and our hands were free. As prisons went — I would learn this eventually from observation and experience — this one was luxurious. After all, we were not being punished. Indeed, we had done nothing wrong, except for misplacing our personhood.

It must have been next to a laundry, because the stench of urine was beyond belief. Every morning a slave from the laundry came to collect our piss as well.

They only fed us once a day, refilling the water and the lone amphora of very weak wine; the bread was stale but plentiful. And all the rats we could catch and roast over the open fire we kept going on the stone floor — a plentiful source of meat.

There was even a running water lavatory on one end, with four openings you could sit over, and our chains were long enough to reach it. But they had to teach me how to use it, and to this day I'd rather squat to shit, and I long to clean myself with leaves and not with a sponge someone else has used before me.

The toilet and the food made this a truly upscale slaves' warehouse. I've since learned how lucky I was.

You've experienced other prisons.
Including this one. You'd think that an actor could be allowed to prepare to play a god in a slightly more luxurious chamber than this!

The woman who had cleaned me up to be raped was

with us. So were others who had been with me on the pirate ship, but the numbers were depleted each day. A few died and were removed. Each day brought new captives, and the sick and dying were removed, as well as some healthy ones. I did not understand the reason.

The woman had a name: Spider. Perhaps it was a nickname. She was, she told me, a weaver. She taught me to say the name: a-RAKH-nê … she had been named in Greek, the language, she told me, of civilized people. "But you must learn Latin, too. At least a few words. Enough to avoid being thought slow-witted."

It seemed she spoke from experience, and that this was not her first time being sold. Her previous owners were Greeks in Cappadocia, a cloth merchant family; the master had been bankrupted and forced to make a quick sale; he had not realized that the buyer was a front for pirates.

"Why do I have to learn two languages?"

"Because you are not going to be sweeping floors or chopping onions," said Spider. "It's true that the lords and masters only speak Latin to the slaves and the lower classes. But among themselves, they affect to speak Greek. They think it makes them seem more refined."

If they already owned the whole world, why did they need to seem more refined? Who were they trying to impress?

"So … your master is called the *dominus*. But when you talk to him, say *domine*. And he will have a wife, even if his taste runs more to your sort. You will call her *domina*. You're not a person, so they can do anything they want to you. In the end, you're just like a table, or a jug of wine. If you find a good house, they may even say they love you. They will expect your love, of course. They've paid for it.

And eventually, if you're thrifty and thoughtful, your peculium will grow and you can even buy back your personhood. And if you're not too shopworn, you could go into business. You could even be a slave dealer; ex-slaves know the business better than anyone. But for now, learn to speak. Sometimes your tongue will be the only thing that saves you from a beating."

"A beating."

"In your case, your tongue may have other uses, too. Keep it agile, and don't do something that will get it cut off."

I hoped to see the centurion again, but I only saw the little Greek, who was a linguist as well as an accountant — that was how he could understand me. He would supervise the deliveries and the removals. From time to time he would have us weighed, and write the results down on his tablet. I understood more and more of what he said but did not dare say anything.

Days came and went. I learned that the tall, black-as-the-night ones were from a territory well south of the empire, and that they were warriors who often made fierce gladiators. The shaggy blond ones often were from Germania, and had a pungent odor, perhaps from anointing themselves with deer fat. There were those called Celts, and there were Scythians, and Jews ... but few of the prisoners save Spider spoke my language — and none of the new additions did. I had come from the very end of the known world.

The day came when they called out Spider to be removed.

I burst into tears and said, "You take me too! She like

mother for me!"

Some of the slaves laughed. I'd made a fool of myself with my bad grammar.

The Greek stopped and peered at me. *"Latine loqueris?"* he said.

"I'm learning. You take her, I no learn no more."

"Greek?"

"Skatá!"

They were all laughing, even the black warriors from the other end of the world. I felt humiliated.

The Greek had a tripod brought in and he sat down. They pulled Spider out and threw her down in front of him. They spoke for a long time; I could not make out all the words, but it seemed that she was telling him something of my story, and something of her own.

After that conversation, he motioned for his assistants to take away about a dozen, but Spider stood there for a moment.

"What happened? What did he say?"

"You're a valuable piece of property," she said. "I'm not. But he is letting me say goodbye at least."

I said to the Greek, "Don't take care — I be more valuable — she teach me speak more good."

"Don't massacre the tongue of the muses," he said in my own language. "I will teach you better than she could. It will hurt, but you will thank me."

And then they took her away. The pirate, the centurion, and now my surrogate mother. I was alone again.

I see you became accustomed to losing anyone you felt attached to.

What do you care? Finish the makeup.

I'm sorry. You distracted me with your story.

But you are right. And so was the centurion Marcus, when he told me not to love.

I was learning this lesson very quickly.

But yourself! You mustn't give up loving yourself.

Loving myself? Perhaps I never have.

V

MIRROR

Spider left me a gift. I suppose she must have found it when collecting her things: everything she owned would belong to her master when she was sold, so she must have talked the Greek into letting me have it.

It was the warped brass plate in which I had first seen my own face.

The Greek, who had a name, it turned out — Aristarchos — treated me better than I expected. He moved me out of the holding area and into a real room. I had never had one of those before, not even when I was free. The room was little more than a cupboard, but it had a raised concrete bed covered with straw and a woolen blanket, and a little oil lamp with an erotic scene. I was still in the warehouse district, but I was not caged with a hundred others.

I could read at night, and Aristarchos made me read *every* night. None of this "Greetings, master! My name is Sporus!" that the average traveller might learn. He said, "You're not going to be the kitchen help. They'll expect you at parties, with society. If someone quotes Ovid to you, and compares you to the virginal Proserpina gathering flowers in the valley, her dress torn by accident to reveal her breast to the predatory God of Hell … you must be swift to answer, snappily: 'usque adeo est properatus amor.' If you say 'Sorry, I beg your pardon, I don't understand,' they will take you for a dumb slave, and you'll have a bloody rear end with nothing to show for it. But understand the art of poetry … seduce the mind, don't just stir the patrician penis … you'll survive, you will even prosper. To a slave, all sex is rape, for even the possibility of consent is forbidden. So you must have the master think you, for a moment, his equal."

"Why would he want that?"

"They all fantasize about that. That all those around them love them, would serve out of sheer devotion without the constant specter of the lash. You must feed that fantasy. You must play whatever role you are given, play as if your life depends on it. But always know it is only a role. It is not you. You must not forget what you are."

"A slave?"

"On an even deeper level," said Aristarchos, "you're still a human being."

Deep into the night, I would pore over the scrolls I had been lent. Worlds were opening up, but in those worlds I was at best half-blind. There were mysteries. The Latin language, the words all categorized, marching in strict military rows, each with its proper ending, walking down its proper pathway … you could say things with a clarity I didn't know language could express. And Greek, so similar in its structures, so different in application! A language designed for ambiguity, where a single change in one vowel in a word could add layers of doubt, hope, or desire; a language with a different dialect for every species of poetry. I found the language very hard, to be sure, but it entranced me.

Removed from the dehumanizing cage of the warehouse, given no chores except my studies, there were times when I didn't think about my enslavement much. The food was simple: porridge, bread, olives, an occasional bit of meat. But I do not think I ate so well in my old life.

Each day my Latin improved. I stumbled over endings and genders, but the verbs had a relentless logic. You could tell why the people who spoke this language ruled the world.

After a time, I could speak after a fashion, and without too barbarous an accent. My Greek, though, not so much; Aristarchos despaired of my ever understanding the second aorist, or the middle voice.

But I was lonely.

I tried to inquire about Spider, to see if she had been sold nearby … no one knew anything. My tutor was not my friend. He had a job to do. Sometimes, just in case I forgot that we weren't friends, he'd treat me to a touch of the strap when I couldn't decline some demonstrative pronoun. But he never drew blood, and I could see it saddened him to beat me. So, I suffered without complaint, thinking that at least I had good food and a real bed, and who knew how long that could last?

Then there were other lessons. Deportment. I had to stand, walk, and sit with grace. This I took to easily. I had been raised by women.

There was the *kithara*. A Greek instrument very conducive to seduction. A single note, once plucked, hung in the air like a lover's sigh.

In addition, there was the *Ars Amatoria* — more Ovid, you see — though my tutor's instruction on this was more theoretical than physical. He never laid a hand on me in that way. I thought that either he really was worried about damaging this "fragile" piece of merchandise, or he was one of those rare individuals without any taste for the same sex whatsoever. People like that do exist … trust me, I've seen everything.

He taught me the different customs among the peoples of the empire; how in Rome the quality of *virtus* or manliness was ascribed only to the penetrator, regardless of who was being penetrated, which meant that well brought up Roman men only exercised their *virtus* on slaves or members of the lower classes, unlike in Greece where love formed a real part of such a relationship; for Romans, it was power over an underling that was the motivating force. He would go on to describe the mating customs among the Celts, the Scythians, the Numidians, the Parthians, and it was all rather exotic but also a bit dull.

When I nodded in those lessons, he didn't punish me. I only got the strap for missing my conjugations.

And one day, after beating me, he took me to the public baths. It was, I supposed, by way of apology. He told me it was a small place, not like the palatial baths in the city. But it was the most overwhelming experience of my life till then. First, the baths themselves — the scorching caldarium, the soothing tepidarium, the bracing frigidarium where slaves kept shovelling in snow brought in from distant hills — a shock to my body but afterwards, I felt so pure, so refreshed. The fact that there was an institution like this, just to keep clean. The hawkers with refreshments. The attendants who seemed to double as prostitutes, sneaking off to the shadows with their clients.

Then there were the bathers — the men, at any rate, for women used the waters at a different hour — some arriving in rags, others in togas, yet underneath we were all the same — senator or fruit vendor. For a time, they left those identities behind and immersed themselves and were at peace.

"And this," Aristarchos said, "is what it means to be civilized. Forget the towering columns, the roads that criss-cross the whole world. Everywhere they go — in Gaul, in Hispania, in Africa, the Romans build baths."

We walked back through the market; I held his belongings for him, and before we got back, he bought me an apple.

Not long after that, I went to Aristarchos's study and found him oddly limping about. One arm was bruised. "What happen?" I asked him.

"*Happened, happened,*" he said.

"How can you correct my grammar when you're in pain?"

"It's nothing," he said. "My master was in a bad mood."

It was only in that moment that I realized that Aristarchos was a slave too, like me. I suppose I should have known. He didn't seem to have a home, or a wife, and his room was in the warehouse area. He was small man, but he seemed ageless. I must have stared at him oddly, because he said, not unkindly, "I suppose you've only just figured it out."

"But … you move about freely. You're not chained up. You go where you please. You could even run away." He laughed bitterly.

"Child … Rome runs on slavery. Our hands and feet and backs build the temples and palaces and aqueducts, of course. But it's the minds of slaves that balance their books, tutor their children, and keep their estates from being mismanaged. Only the lowest are in chains of iron, but there are many other kinds of chains. Why am I still a slave? I'm a wonderful accountant, and I can expound on literature and art at the best of dinner parties, but I cannot manage my own peculium."

I hoped I would do better. Any abuse could be endured if freedom lay at the end of the path.

"Now, Sporus, tomorrow you and I will soon be parting ways. Oh, do not look sad! I know you think you can't get to know anyone before they disappear from your life, but this will end soon. I have made a financial arrangement with the steward of a great house. He will pay a price that is acceptable to my master, as the agent of the state which in principle acquired you as contraband when the pirate ship and its cargo were seized. Even I will benefit; I have taught you well enough to replenish my peculium. Until the next time I get drunk and gamble," he added ruefully. "Or wake up in a brothel, having lost everything."

"What great house?" I asked him. "Is it the Emperor?"

"Ha! It seems like only yesterday that you knew of nothing but a few huts and forests and now you're talking about the Emperor! No, but I assure you, you will almost certainly see your God in person. I have heard that he visits this great house on occasion."

I couldn't resist. Seeing him like this, afflicted yet still thinking of my welfare, I went up to him and hugged him, as though he were my own father, whom I had never known.

"Haven't I told you not to love anyone?" he said brusquely. But he didn't rebuff my embrace.

Looking into his eyes, I could intuit that there was another reason why he had not tried to use me in that way. He had finely honed features. Though his eyes were lined, his face had a delicacy to it, a boyish quality; it was that in him that had seemed ageless. And I suddenly understood … "Where I'm going," I said, "you've already been, haven't you?"

He didn't answer. I went on … "And your inability to hold on to your peculium … it's got something to do with that, hasn't it? There's a darkness that gnaws at you, deep inside. That is always telling you you're no more than … an object."

Aristarchos said, "You have seen."

Like the plate of warped bronze Spider had given me, this man, too, was a mirror. We were each other's mirror, gazing across the gulf of time.

But mirrors can deceive. "I'll never be defeated," I said. "I'll do what I did to my previous life — I'll wall it away, untouchable, forever. I won't lose my soul."

Your life, on the other hand…
Oh, be quiet. Will this makeup never be done?
Patience, goddess. What does time mean to an immortal?
I'm not an immortal *yet*.

But after your performance, your masterpiece, you will be....

VI

MARKET

Nothing is as pointless as the chatter of slaves.

I've heard that saying so many times during the past four reigns. Yet here I am, chattering to a slave, pouring out my deepest inner pain as one might pour a libation from the dregs of a loving-cup.

Say what you will, Goddess. Tomorrow I'll be making someone else up. These scenes from mythology — fabulae crepidatae — have become all the rage in our entertainment ... dare I call it such ... industry. Tomorrow I'll do Hercules ripping up his wife and children ... or Medea cutting up her little brother into pieces and throwing him overboard. You're getting it easy, being raped to death; my makeup will make you such a delicate flower that the crowd might even root for you, and beg whatever monstrous Gaul or Nubian they've assigned to play Pluto to spare you ... who knows, you might even get a thumbs up. Not.

You're quite the chatterbox.

Only because you're not telling me more.

Show me a mirror.

Must I?

Oh! I am hideous! You have made me a clown, not a goddess.

Because, Your Divinity, you must shine even in the uppermost rows of the Circus, where the slaves sit. As for where the Emperor sits, he's probably already acquainted with your face — and other parts of your anatomy.

Oh, you lowly little hairdresser ... how well you know how to hurt a girl. Just to shut you up ... I will tell what happened next.

The next day, I was summoned to Aristarchos's room and told to strip. Two hefty men flanked the accountant. They were both twice my size and amply proportioned. One of them took my tunica and tossed it into a brazier. I started to panic. Surely these men were not here to ... soften me up for my next master! ... a whimper escaped my throat, but Aristarchos laughed. Presently two women came in — they too were giantesses — and between them they carried a wooden chest topped with a gold ornament of lions' heads facing in opposite directions. When they opened the chest I saw ... cloth. And a glint of gold.

Aristarchos said, "Didn't we pick the barbarian prince story?"

"We haven't picked a story."

"A slave with your looks must come with a story. I thought you knew that."

"I came from a village at the edge of the world."

"No, no, a palace. A palace at the edge of the world."

The two men began pouring olive oil on me and rubbing me down. I confess it felt good. Sensual. Not like being shoved about like a feelingless doll. I was embarrassed and looked for something to conceal my obvious pleasure.

Aristarchos laughed again. "You can keep a little of the coyness," he said. "They will find it endearing. But it's good to see they haven't completely destroyed your ability to feel."

When they were through with the anointing, they scraped the oil off with strigils, leaving my skin tingling. "And now they will dress you," said my tutor. And one of the women beckoned me with a finger. She reached into the chest and pulled a garment of a material so soft and diaphanous it seemed to have been woven from spider-webs, making me think of the woman who had been like a mother to me for a short time.

When the garment touched my skin it was more like a caress.

"I can see," the woman said, "you have never felt the touch of silk before." She launched into a fantastical tale about how this fabric is woven from the sputum of caterpillars....

Meanwhile the other woman — did I forget to say? — though they were a matched pair, those impressive women, one of them was pale as snow and even her eyes were bleached and a little pink, while the other was so black, her skin was almost a shiny, deep blue, like a night sky in the moonlight. Had they scoured the earth for such a pair? Surely the Romans could bring to life any marvel a poet could dream of. They were pleasingly plump and I found myself daydreaming about returning to infancy and suckling at one of their generous bosoms.

In short, being cleaned and dressed was humiliating in a different way from when people were chaining me up and beating me. Luckily, once I had on the silk tunica, and a blue chlamys also of silk which was fastened with a fibula of real gold, I no longer betrayed any arousal.

"You look like a proper, aristocratic Greek boy," Aristarchos said, "perhaps from the north, with your hair color."

"Is this to help with the story about my being a captured prince?"

Aristarchos said, "Greece, motherland of culture, hasn't had an aristocracy in a century or two; the best of us are slaves now." And he looked away. I think he had a tear in his eye. "But no," he said. "You're not being decked out like a prince for some special show. Where you are going, everything and every*one* is beautiful. From the house slaves to the gardener, there is nothing in that house that is not purest elegance."

I found myself being carried in a litter, with Aristarchos accompanying me. The litter-bearers moved swiftly, in tandem, and with a kind of precision that made the ride far smoother than an oxcart. The curtains were drawn and I didn't see much — though I heard and smelled plenty.

The smells of Ostia! Human sweat, perfume, bread baking in ovens open to the streets, but through it all the smell of shit — horse, ox, human — pervading everything.

"Rome will smell worse," Aristarchos said.

"I want to look," I said, putting my hand on the curtain.

"Yes, yes, but not here. I don't want you to see —" It was too late. I was peeking out and we were just passing a slave auction. It was a small square with a temporary auction platform set up, and salesmen yelling out from all four corners of the platform, several auctions running at the same time, and bids frantically coming from all sides.

I saw a burly man with wild, orange hair, being prodded

and poked by a potential buyer.

"A Celt," said Aristarchos.

I saw a boy and girl my own age being twirled around like a matched pair of dolls. I heard a barker call out: "One hundred sesterces! Do I hear two? Three hundred sesterces!" I would have thought a year's supply of bread and wine to be a high price, but I heard higher, too.

You could tell the slaves from the free people in just two ways. They were naked. Some were not even chained. Perhaps they were already domesticated, not war captives, or born into slavery and so knew nothing else. I thought I saw Spider, but I could not be sure. It must be her, surely. She looked at me. She seemed to be about to say something, but her keeper shoved her up to the block.

I heard another barker shout "Five thousand! Fifty-five hundred!" and I saw that the object being sold was someone little different from me. Young, and extremely frightened. But exquisite. This might indeed be the captive princeling that I was pretending to be. And his price was going up and up.

"Close the curtain!" Aristarchos whispered.

"Why is he so expensive?" I said.

I think he met my eye. I am not sure, he was so distant. I wouldn't forget the look in his eye very easily. Hot tears spurted, wetting my cheeks.

"Pueri delicati are highly desired by the best families," Aristarchos said. "After a while, the barker might have to stop counting in sesterces and move up to denarii. Perhaps even aurei. Or the numbers will go off the end of the scribe's tablet."

"How much was paid for me?"

"I don't know," he said. Though perhaps he did, and

simply did not want me to get an inflated sense of myself. "Draw the curtain."

I would have done so immediately, but at that moment, some blood spattered on my face. The litter had been moving and my eyes were level with someone's crucified feet. They had used nails. I looked up at the wretch. The cross was low. This was the moment when, his lungs collapsing from the asphyxiation, he had sort of crumpled up and expired, straining at the nails to produce a few final spurts of blood. A bird was sitting on his shoulder, pecking at an eye.

Quickly, I closed the curtain.

But the thing that struck me the most was this: a main was dying in agony in the middle of the street ... and no one was even stopping to look. It was a sight so commonplace that people were just going about their business.

They'll look at you *all right. You're such a celebrity.*

And somehow, it's more satisfying to watch awful things happen to a celebrity. I was their Empress for a while. Was I not loved? Nero was loved, though it is no longer fashionable to say so.

We never talk about past Emperors. If we did, we could end up where you've ended up, reenacting one of the great moments of myth or history.

Thank you for reminding this goddess of her fate.

I'm sure you don't need reminding. But at least, for the more subtle entertainment value of your life's story, you have an attentive audience of one. So carry on, Daughter of Demeter.

Let me tell you what happened when I closed the silken curtain...

VII

OXCART

And what happened when you closed the curtain?
So you *do* want me to go on.
Of course I do. You're the least boring job I've had since the Kalends.

... in essence, nothing. I drew the curtains closed, and I shut out the world with its noise, squalor, beauty, and pain. And we went on in silence for a while longer.

Until I asked, suddenly realizing that I hadn't actually asked ... "Are we going to Rome?"

He said, "Who is there in this empire who is *not* going to Rome? Rome is the center of the world."

The outskirts of Ostia are a scant five *mille passuum* from the outskirts of Rome. I thought I would be riding by litter all the way, but at the inland boundary of Ostia we were switched to an oxcart. For the rest of the afternoon, things were arriving and being loaded into the cart; for I was just one of the pieces of costly merchandise that had been listed for delivery to my new master's house. It was a marvel that I was still not chained up. Though where would I have run to?

Other carts joined us as well. Presently there was a convoy, but mine was first in the line. A line of slaves came bearing more and more goods.

There were large amphorae filled with wine and olive oil. There were bolts of cloth. There was a monkey in a cage. There was another slave, too, a strapping specimen in a loincloth. Perhaps a gladiator. He was quite heavily chained, and snarled and snapped like a wild beast. He spoke in grunts. There was also a sloe-eyed woman, quite exotic-looking.

Aristarchos kept making notes on his tablet.

There was glassware, exquisitely transparent in iridescent hues. There were wine cups — Greek ones, painted with all manner of mythical or erotic imagery. Some showed voluptuous women, some boys like me, with the legend *ho pais kalos* … yes, I was already starting to pick out a word or two. And a silver one as well, in which I saw, for the first time, what exactly it was that a *puer delicatus* did, for the cup depicted in relief, a person much like me, nude, reclining on a couch and being subjected to the attentions of a man in a toga; the cup left little to the imagination. I looked at it and I was very afraid.

I looked at Aristarchos, who was climbing off the cart now that I had been deposited with the cargo. I think there was a tear in my eye, and he did not look directly at me; I fear there may have been one in his, as well.

He stood by the side of the cart, his face peering up past the wooden edge, still not meeting my gaze. He said softly, "It's not a bad life. You will taste a lot of rare viands that ordinary mortals can't dream of trying. You'll know the private nicknames of senators and poets. And if there is pain, it can be dulled by poppy juice, or by a tea made from willow bark; the steward will know how to find such things. And no one will strike you, at least not enough to draw blood. No one would dare to damage your skin. Did I say the steward? You will meet him soon, and I must finally leave you."

He turned, but before doing so he tossed me a coin. "Another bit of change for your peculium," he said.

And he walked away without so much as a *vale*. Perhaps it would have been too painful.

I looked at the coin. It was a sestertius and it was shiny and big, fresh from the mint. And by now, I could read the legend:

NERO CLAVD CAESAR AVG GER PM TRP PP

A bold portrait: a young man with chubby cheeks, quite a jaw on him; a bit of a sneer; a long neck. I compared it with the other coin in my pouch. The new one was larger and less shiny. Marcus had only given me a dupondius, worth half, and made of bright orichalcum, not bronze.

I was alone again, and two military men were riding up to us.

To my great joy, one of them was the centurion who had been kind to me after the sea-battle with the pirates.

"Marce!" I called out.

He ignored me, and went on talking to his companion.

I started to call his name again, but the other soldier gave me a clout with his quirt. It stung but left no mark — he had been skillful.

"Impudent cunt!" he said. To Marcus, he said, "Shall I kill the *cinaedus*, sir?"

Marcus waved him away. Some soldiers on foot came up and took their places in front of and behind the cart. Marcus's torso loomed over me and his horse stuck its head in the cart, perhaps looking for a snack among the bags of fruit. He glared at the handful of people in the cart until they all cast their eyes down ... all but me. Then his demeanor changed quite abruptly. He winked at me, and said, "Your Latin has improved."

"Oh! You notice me say 'Marce' and no 'Marcus," I said in my best barbarian accent.

He laughed. "Infelicities are charming from your lips," he said. "Though if you were in school, you'd get a proper lashing."

I said, "But Aristarchos said if I don't speak proper Greek and Latin I will be a miserable failure."

"I doubt that," he said. "But you could always say nothing at all. That could also be seen as adorable. Perhaps they will think you are a mute, and they will start spilling their secrets. The cost of your silence could add considerably to your peculium ... as would the price of your blabbing!"

"How will I know if I should tell or not tell?"

"If you are right, you will survive. If not —" A throat-slitting gesture. "And I am sure you will understand why I cannot behave towards you as I did when we were at sea. Society would not approve, not here, at the center of the world."

"What's a *cinaedus?*" I asked him.

"You'll know soon enough," he said.

"Centurion!" One of the soldiers was approaching. 'We are ready to escort the cargo into the city."

Marcus immediately became stern again, and acting as though I did not exist. His subordinate saluted him. The foot soldiers formed and began a slow, precise march. Their footfalls on the flat Roman road were a percussive accompaniment to our journey. The carts groaned under the weight of merchandise. My teeth rattled with each turn of the iron wheels.

After what seemed an age of jogging and bumping we reached the walls of the city, just before sunset.

We stopped.

At that stage, Marcus returned, and when we were alone, I asked what the matter was.

"We have to wait until the tenth hour," he said. "No wheeled vehicles in Rome until night. Rome is not a grand place of wide avenues. It started as a village, and the streets are as they were eight hundred years ago. Traffic would bring Rome to its knees if carts and pedestrians shared the roads."

And so came a time of waiting. I had not emptied my bowels and I was feeling desperate. I would have gone by the roadside, but I did not know if that was the kind of thing that got you a beating.

I was weary. I think I was asleep when we started to move again. But coming half awake, I did see the mother of all cities, steeped in gloom. We passed tall wooden structures reeking of human waste. From an open doorway, a fat prostitute jiggled and beckoned.

Wood gave way to concrete and stone. Temples in the starlight, their steps half lit, half shadowed. A statue of a goddess. A triumphal archway, then down another alley.

A link-boy, torch aloft, guided litter-bearers through the street, so narrow that it seemed the opposing walls might bend and touch. The streets not straight but often veering in odd directions. And now, the carts strained as we moved uphill. Soldiers helped to push. I had heard that Rome has seven hills, but had not *felt* that.

Even so, the regular thud of the soldiers' caligae lulled me, made me drift off to sleep. I dreamed....

Of what?
Am I to take nothing private to the grave?
Suit yourself.
I dreamed of a village.
I dreamed of a palace.
My many pasts were weaving into some new fantasy.

When I awoke again it was because the pounding of the military escort's boots on the road abruptly stopped.

There was a wall. We had practically collided with it. In the dark, the wall went beyond the edge of my vision in both directions.

Marcus rode up to me. "This is your home now," he said. Then he rode away.

All I could feel now was terror.

VIII

STORYTELLER

There was, as I have said, a wall. The wall itself was nothing fancy. Indeed, in the light of uplifted torches, I saw that the wall was quite filthy. It even had graffiti, including a crude sketch of a woman tied to a stake, being ravaged by wolves — a common enough sight, I was to learn, in the arena, for the Romans are as cruel as they are civilized.

And in the wall was an ordinary door, which opened. At once came well-trained slaves, all wearing identical tunicae, each knowing exactly what to do as they unloaded the carts and carried the precious objects do into the house.

A tall, thin old man in a tunic and a woollen himation emerged. He looked hither and thither and spotted me. "Come down from there," he said. "He'll want to look at you right away."

Marcus was nowhere to be seen.

The man motioned for a boy to hold up a torch. He looked me over very thoroughly. My teeth. Even felt my privates, perhaps to make sure I had any.

"You'll do," he said. "I'll take you in directly."

"Shouldn't I —" I looked imploringly; he must have known I needed to relieve myself.

"Yes, yes, boy. We have a private shitter. Take care of yourself. We need to make the right impression." He turned to the slaves. "Everything is to be taken to the storage rooms for cataloguing and checking against the master list. Yes, slaves, too. Except this one."

I climbed out and he pushed me forward by the neck. I found myself in the doorway. With some trepidation, I stepped inside the house. A huge black man guarded the door. He was naked, and his feet were chained ... though I noticed that the other end of the chain was not actually attached to anything. The chain was just for show.

"Is this the new one, Croesus?" he asked the tall man.

"Don't be impertinent," came the reply. To me he said, "The *latrina* is to your left. When you are done, go straight to the triclinium. Follow the chatter and you will find it by yourself. Hop to it."

I looked up.

First ... it was a house of the utmost simplicity. I don't know what I was expecting — probably a lot of gold, ornate decorations, colorful statues. Fidgety mosaics and garish murals. But no. Instead there was the impression of spaciousness. The ceiling of the hall was high; a wide stairway led to an upper level.

The foyer was bare except for the masks of dead ancestors. There were columns and past them you could see the atrium, again laid out with simple elegance, with just a single statue of a young boy, very archaic looking — I learned later it was a thousand years old and pilfered from Greece. Above the garden was only starlight. I knew they were unloading the carts, and carrying things inside, but all I had eyes for was this magnificent emptiness.

The toilet was remarkable in that it had but a single opening, allowing you to defaecate in solitary splendor. Surely that, and not the opulent simplicity of the hallway, was what proved how rich the master of this house must be.

The floor of the latrina was a mosaic of an ocean scene. Neptune with his trident, sea creatures — shellfish, squid, a giant octopus all done with such cunning it seemed I was sitting at the ocean's edge.

A torch burned in a bracket, lighting up the bucket with the sponge on a stick with which to clean myself. I was just swabbing at my rear when I heard a voice. I almost jumped out of my skin because there was some kind of acoustic effect that made it sound almost as though the speaker were sitting alongside me.

It came from a nearby room. It was a rounded, modulated voice, and it was telling a story, and it was the most extraordinary Latin I had ever heard — for it was clearly of the utmost literary quality, yet it was also plain-spoken, as common folk talk, so even I could catch the gist of it ...

"'Erras,' inquit, 'Encolpi, si putas contingere posse, ut ante moriaris....'

I translated as best I could into my own language: 'You're wrong, Encolpius, if you think I'm gonna let you get away with dying before me, I'm going to kill myself. I've been looking for a sword. If I hadn't found you, I'd have thrown myself off a cliff ...'"

I was taking a crap in the palace of a rich stranger — why, this personal toilet was as large as my village home had been — listening to the most astonishing tale, in the most beautiful, powerful language. The story went on. It seemed to be about a lovers' quarrel, between a master and slave, but there was more to it than master and slave because it seemed that the slave was adept at acting the dominus, and presently the slave was pretending to cut his own throat with a razor he knew to be blunted, inflaming his possessor's passion still further....

I knew I should hurry.

At that moment, a large man stumbled into the latrina, accompanied by a young slave. I could not see him that clearly in the light from the one torch and in any case he had drawn his toga over his face.

"I thought this toilet was supposed to be private," he said.

"It is, domine," said the slave. He gestured at me to finish my business.

"Wipe your arse at once," the man growled. "Or I'll puke on your head." His slave held up a feather and was about to tickle his throat. In a minute, my fine silk tunica was going to be hurled on.

Hurriedly, I cleaned myself up and left the lavatory through another door. As soon as I closed it, that mellifluous voice returned, narrating more of the tale. It was even louder now, bouncing off the four walls of the atrium, amplified and echoing on marble surfaces.

I found myself in the cloister that ran all the way around the atrium. It was dark save for the occasional lit torches, but I could hear that voice, and the story he told was riveting. I presently found myself at the entrance to a triclinium. A dozen guests reclined on couches. Shyly, I stood at the opening, not wanting this miracle of storytelling to cease.

I looked at the narrator, who was reading from a scroll. He wore simple dress — simple as the house itself, yet bespeaking immense wealth — a plain, white toga, though it was the finest wool, a cloak dipped in purple held in place by a gold fibula. He wore a wreath. Was this the emperor himself? Surely not ... this was not the pudgy face on the two coins in my pouch. This was someone quite refined-looking, a man in his forties, perhaps, who had taken great pains with his grooming and makeup.

On the table were dishes I could never even imagine. Giant stuffed birds and the heads of unknown beasts. Fruits I had never seen. The guests had not seen me come in, so entranced were they by their host's narration.

Two naked boys, with little wings strapped on, were tending to the guests, sitting first in one lap then another, or being idly stroked, like kittens. They giggled, they smiled, they purred. Was this to be my job in this household?

The host went on: *"And Eumolpus, the poet, had not bothered to interrupt our death-scene ...* ah, but I see someone else has."

The two *pueri delicati* looked up at me. Beautiful they were indeed, and yet — their eyes looked daggers. I stared at the ground, not daring to meet their gaze. Had I arrived in some kind of competition, where boys too knowing for their age played games to curry favor with a fickle master? I knew that my terror on entering the house was justified.

"Who is this bewitching creature?" said the master of the house. "Croesus, do tell."

"But you already know, master," said the steward in Greek. For that was who the thin old man was. He had suddenly appeared behind me as though by magic.

"Approach him, you little brat," he hissed at me.

The dominus crooked a finger. Awkwardly, I came closer.

"You speak Latin?" he said.

"Ita, domine."

"Greek?"

"Me not talking Greek so good, master."

"From *your* lips, child, that travesty sounds like Sappho!" And then he said to the others: *"Eros daut' etinaxen emoi phrenas, anemos kat oros drysin empeson."* And, as they all applauded, he translated it into Latin, looking into my eyes: *"Eros shook my heart, like a mountain wind that sweeps down on an oak-tree."* And I admit I blushed ... I mean, my cheeks went hot and cold and I shivered all over. He motioned for me to come closer.

He sat me on the couch next to him. "Off with this girlish silk," he said to me, and ripped my tunica away so quickly I had not time to get even more embarrassed. Dipping a cloth in a kylix of resinated white wine, he wiped my face. "Nor does your face need painting. I did not buy you to be a whore." The resin stung my nostrils. I sneezed. "We already have enough of those in this house. Be still. I shall not eat you. Not tonight, anyway," he added, then, seeing that I was about to burst into tears, he relented. Sensing there was kindness in him, I hugged him, and shed more tears into his expensive cloak. "There, there," he said, patting my back. He unclasped his cloak — which I know cost more than I did — and put it around my shoulders. "Perhaps you'd care for a peacock's brain?" And then he started feeding me from a platter on the table.

I had not eaten anything since morning. I swallowed the entire brain; I would later learn that this morsel was worth as much as a week's bread for some peasant.

I did not even know my master's name.

But I was emboldened, and I said, "That story you were telling ... is it true? Who are Giton, and Encolpius, and Eumolpus?"

"We all have an epic inside us," my master said, "though we do not always have the leisure to write it. In my case, I daresay I shall not live to finish it."

You were sold to Gaius Petronius Arbiter?

You guessed.

Who would not have guessed it by now? And to think you heard his writing from his own lips — while crapping, no less! His unfinished epic is a legend. And even more so, the letter he wrote to the Emperor Nero before he committed —

Don't speak ill of my husband.

Ex-husband! You've had two others.

And none to hold a candle. Let me tell you what else Petronius said.

For indeed, as I was to learn by morning, I was now the property of Petronius Arbiter, one of the most celebrated wits in history. A man whose entire life was a poem. A man whose taste in music, painting, sculpture, poetry, drama, and the art of love, was such that the Emperor called him his *arbiter of elegance.* But it was not until I left his service that I was to appreciate just how important he was.

But now, the man whose name I did not yet know was saying, "My nephew, Vinicius, wrote me a letter in which he said the resemblance is uncanny. What do you all think? Lucan?"

A dour man on a nearby coach said, "Uncanny, indeed, uncanny."

"Seneca?"

Another, even more dour, muttered something.

I heard others, mumbling the same thing.

"Excuse me, *domine*," I said. "I am just an impertinent boy but ... who is it I resemble so uncannily?"

Petronius said, "Resemblance is, indeed the issue. I think that it is just about exact. Exact, of course —" he gave me a playful prod — "there are some anatomical anomalies. But why have perfection when you can have *better* than perfect? I would not be surprised, Sporus, if the one person who is to judge just how *uncanny* the resemblance is ... were to prefer you to the real thing."

We all heard footsteps. Tottering, unsteady. A man stood at the entrance to the triclinium, his arm on the shoulder of a slave. It was the man who had been vomiting in the lavatory not long before. Now, in the light of many torches, I saw his features more clearly. He was broad-faced, broad-shouldered, and his hair resembled an upside-down wine bowl. His slave was wiping the last specks of vomitus from his lips.

It amused me to notice that he was using the same sponge that I had earlier used to wipe my posterior.

"Now," said Petronius, "stand up. Pull my purple himation about your shoulders. Here, I'll fix the fibula. Stand up straight and majestic. Put your arms out in a supplicatory gesture and whisper seductively 'Otho, Otho.'"

I got up from the couch and did what I was told. It was, I suppose, my theatrical debut.

"Marcus Salvius Otho," said Gaius Petronius Arbiter. "Who is it that you see before you?"

"Otho, Otho," I said.

The guests drew a collective breath. Something was going on in their minds. Not for the last time in my life, I was playing a role that my audience understood well, but meant nothing to me.

Marcus Salvius Otho looked at me for a long time. He squinted. He peered. He whispered into his slave's ear and the slave whispered something back. He *transformed*. I swear, he actually sobered up on the spot. He became a different person. Heroic, perhaps. A little henpecked as well. He stared at me, he saw *me*, just as I was ... and yet there was someone else here too, someone whose outward soma I was borrowing, though perhaps my soul was still my own.

He gazed at me through this miasma of epiphany and disbelief. "Poppaea?" he whispered.

Then he fainted.

IX
SYMPOSIUM

Although Marcus Salvius Otho had collapsed onto the floor, slaves still managed to drag him to an empty couch. They loosened the folds of his toga, daubed his face with cold water, and the two *delicati* took turns stimulating him in various ways, but he seemed to have passed out for the night.

"We shall ignore him," said Petronius, "but at least now we know that our Sporus is the real thing ... he can even fool the husband."

"But who is Poppaea, *domine*?" I asked.

I don't know why, but it seemed permissible to address my lofty master almost as though I were not his property. I had already learned that this was not the usual way things went in the Romans' world.

"You're not very slavish," Petronius said. "Most would look at the floor, and wince if spoken to, to ward off the inevitable slap. You were not born a slave. Perhaps you *are* a captive prince ... I believe that was the story we were sold on ... along with an unnecessary doubling of the price."

"Nevertheless, *domine*," I persisted, "Who *is* she?"

"Before I answer," Petronius said, "let me explain something. Tomorrow, before breakfast, Croesus will take you to the back and give you ten lashes, for all your saucy back talk — that is not appropriate to my *dignitas* as your master. But I will tell him not to damage your skin, so it will not hurt much. And you do need to learn that, kind as I am, I do own you. Every piece of you. Your pretty little mouth, your radiant hair, your weasley excuse for a *phallos*, and even your empty little mind which I shall hope to fill with thoughts as beautiful as your body. I am not saying this to hurt you, child; I am just telling you the simple truth, the way the world works. For I, too, have a master. And when he whistles, I too must dance. So learn to be more circumspect, especially in front of guests."

Seneca scoffed. "You're too softhearted, Petronius."

"Let him be," Lucan said. "He is eccentric in how he treats his belongings, but it works. His slaves adore him. Do yours?"

"The love of a slave is innate hypocrisy. It's fear, made palatable with an excess of sweet sauce."

"By Juno! Am I not to rule in my own house?" Petronius said. "Summon the steward!"

Croesus was there, kneeling, and I had not even seen him come in. That's how the slaves were in the house — never visible until the moment they were needed. It was an art I would need to master.

"Croesus," Petronius said, "I've sentenced the new boy to ten lashes."

"Very good, *domine*," he said without any visible emotion.

"However, seeing that he is something of a chatterbox,

I'll give him until dawn to talk me out of it."

"A veritable Solomon!" said a bearded young man with a covered head.

"Whoever that might be," Petronius said, beckoning me to sit beside him once more, and stuffing another peacock's brain into my mouth, though the heavy admixture of garum and honey in the sauce was too confusing to my tongue.

"An ancient king of my old country," said the young man.

"And you, too, are now a king, young Agrippa, since your father was murdered while watching the games in Caesarea," Seneca said. "Yet you do not rule. You just sit around in Rome, frittering away your private treasury, while our praefectus handles law and order."

Petronius said, "You're as Roman as we are, Marcus Julius Agrippa, known to the subjects you haven't seen in ages as King Herod the not-so-Great . But we are in a Symposium, and you must recite poetry."

Slaves poured more wine. The *delicati* moved from couch to couch.

"Where is the Lady Poppaea?" I asked, since if I was to be "lightly" beaten in the morning, I might as satisfy all my questions.

"There are no ladies here," Petronius said. "I told you, it's a Symposium, not a dinner-party. A sober evening of edification and poetry."

"But there's a lady over there," I said, indicating one. Looking again, I saw that it was not a lady at all, but a rather grotesquely made-up elderly gentleman, his face completely white with lead paint.

The guests all began laughing. I had made a fool of

myself so many times that evening that I wanted to shrivel up into the floor.

"Sit," Petronius said. "We'll have more poetry." A slave served wine from a dipper of purple crystal.

Presently it was Lucan's turn to begin a recitation, and although my master's eyes were opened, his mind seemed vacant. It seemed he understood the art of sleeping through a full performance without ever appearing to drift. I, however, did start to fall asleep. It had been a day of changes, and in this bewildering household, I had no idea of my true place. I was sitting, practically in the lap of the master of the house, who presently, slightly stirring, made me try a lark's tongue, then a young dormouse roasted in honey, all delicacies I could barely dream of; yet I knew I was going to be whipped in the morning. Who were these people, who could torment you and lavish sweetmeats on you, all in one breath?

"So this is what it means to be rich," I said. "Slaves everywhere, and all-night banquets."

"This isn't a banquet," Petronius said. "It's just a symposium. Soon, you'll see what a real banquet is. If you think this is extravagant ... and I am by far the most refined and tasteful of those I know. Why ... in my book, I describe *such* a banquet — but you shall read it for yourself. Once you are properly trained. Because at the moment, you are a ravishment to the eye, but to the ear ... that is another matter. That fool of a tutor has taught you almost nothing. And as for the *ars amatoria* ... of that you know nothing and you will need at least some rudiments if you're going to have a successful career — and help me recoup my investment.."

There came a familiar voice from the doorway of the

triclinium: "Uncle!"

And I was amazed to see that it was my friend — if a slave could be said to *have* friends — Marcus, the centurion.

"I've done the whole inventory, Uncle," he said. "You are now the owner of some of the most beautiful things in Rome."

He had interrupted Seneca in mid-narration, but some in the company seemed actually relieved. Though I knew more Latin than Greek, I hadn't understood much of it.

To the guests, Petronius said, "You know, of course, my nephew Marcus Vinicius. Most beloved by the gods, and always in the heart of his extremely doting Uncle, Gaius Petronius Arbiter. Quite the soldier, for so young a man. About to be raised to *tribunus*, I understand, though he entered the Divine Emperor's service as a mere centurion, wishing to taste an ordinary soldier's rough life, the Gods alone know why. And, being my nephew, he also has exquisite taste in poetry."

I was beginning to have an inkling of the complexity of this aristocrat whom I'd had the audacity to think of as a friend.

"My slave," said Petronius, "reminds me of the true purpose of this evening's gathering. It's time to get to the real business of our symposium. What will the topic of tonight's discourse be?"

"Love," said the old man garbed as a woman.

"Tragedy," said Seneca the tragedian.

"Democracy," said Lucan. The guests at the party gasped.

"All of these subjects flirt with destiny," Petronius said. "You, Lucan, will probably be ordered to commit suicide one of these days; I doubt you'll live to see thirty, if you keep pining for the Republic. And as for tragedy, we're surrounded by it; why wallow? And love — well, just look at *you*," he said to the man in a stola. "Can you do a better job than Plato?"

"I have a subject," said Marcus Vinicius, and he got me from his uncle's couch, led me by the hand to the centre of the circle, and slipped off the purple cloak that had been my only covering. "Let's talk about beauty." To me, he whispered, "Just stand there, looking a little stand-offish, unattainable. Be their muse. Yes, let them stare. You're an object. But at least you're a valuable one."

He let go. I was the center of attention.

Behind me was the door to the triclinium. In front was the couch where my master sat. Behind him there was a mural, women dancing among trees.

To hide my embarrassment, I looked at the trees in the murals. I started to count the leaves. They were so realistically rendered that it was easy to imagine myself in that grove as well, dancing among the nymphs.

"May I begin," said Marcus, "by quoting a poem by Asklepiades, where he says *ei kathyperthe labois khrysea ptera...* imagine if you had golden wings and a quiver on your silvery shoulders ... if you stood next to Cupid in all his splendor ... could his mother Venus tell you apart? ..." He winked at me, and then it was someone else's turn to discuss the nature of beauty. Which they did at length, quoting poets to prove their points. Their topics ranged from fragility to impermanence, from spirituality to physicality, and then, too, they would discuss every piece of my anatomy as though I weren't even there.

Agrippa spoke next, and he chose to speak some odd,

guttural language. He translated it, though: *"Your lips drop sweetness as the honeycomb, my bride; milk and honey are under your tongue* ... It is from our holy scriptures," he said. "You did ask me who Solomon was. And before you ask, these words describe a woman." A few oohs and aahs at this anomaly.

"Your religious texts seem rather erotic," said Lucan, "not unlike Ovid. Are your gods fertility gods?"

"We only have one," Agrippa said.

"Heavens, only one," Seneca said. "No wonder we crushed you. Hardly seems fair. Now, as for fair, consider young Sporus's eyelashes..."

They went on in this vein for a while, eulogizing my eyes, my nose, my smile, and many words were expended on my buttocks, while I stood stiffly, feeling quite humiliated.

And presently Otho began twisting and murmuring, and it was clear he was about to emerge from his stupor. One of the slaves emptied a jug filled with water chilled with snow — *that* must have been expensive — on his head. He sat up all at once. He saw me. He interrupted the chorus of encomiums, crudely calling out "Poppaea! Poppaea!" and shambling off the couch to enfold me in his beastly, fat, vomit-stained arms. He did not quite make it and fell, prostrate at my feet, with a groan.

The audience applauded. "With the fewest words," Seneca said, "he has said the most! What delicious irony, to praise the absent love while staring at the one organ she does not possess!" They were all laughing, and I still had no idea who Poppaea might be.

"He has won!" cried Lucan. "No one else shall be the victor!"

"Indeed. His rhetoric has outdone you all," Petronius said. The slaves pressed a laurel wreath on Otho's head and lifted him up — half pushed, half pulled him back to his couch. He had passed out again.

The guests began to get ready to leave, with slaves adjusting their clothing, straightening their togas, pinning their cloaks, and presenting them with little gifts as souvenirs of the evening. And presently there was no one left but myself, Marcus Vinicius, and a snoring Marcus Salvius Otho.

Marcus (my Marcus) said, "We'd better put him in the guest cubiculum."

"Sporus will bring his breakfast in the morning," Petronius said.

"I'd love to see Otho's face when he looks upon our Poppaea sober. But I need to go back to the castra. I shall leave you with your latest acquisition." And he left, without even bothering to glance at his uncle's property.

I was still standing there, feeling a strange combination of emotions: a warmth, even a kind of pride, that so many wealthy men had been singing my praises, but also a stark terror because I had been in this house for only a few hours, and knew I was completely at the mercy of one man.

Slaves were snuffing out the lamps and carrying away the half-eaten remains of the cena. "You can attend me in the bath," he said, "and in the bedchamber, for the rest of the night, though I daresay it is coming up to dawn. You'll have plenty of time to convince me not to have you beaten."

He had not forgotten! At these words my fear became so palpable that I almost threw up ... what with the rich foods and the unaccustomed amount of wine that had been fed me. For was this not the reason I had been purchased — so that some rich lord could brutalize me in degradation and pain?

"What's the matter, Sporus? You're shaking like a leaf." He called to his steward. "Croesus — take the creature to the cubiculum and instruct him."

Instruct me? Had I not had enough instruction in my role from that crucified pirate? "No, domine, no!" I exclaimed as the terror seized hold of me completely and I broke down in a paroxysm of weeping.

X
CUBICULUM

"There now," said my master. "Tears *can* be a way to avoid the whip, but when a master has a bit of cruel streak, tears might encourage *more* whipping...."

Croesus took me by the shoulder ... quite roughly, after the tenderness which his owner had shown me ... and marched me away, while Petronius sipped at a posset that one of his women had just poured for him.

First, Croesus took me to the slaves' quarters. They were not as ghastly as the place in Ostia where we had been warehoused, but they were a reminder that I hadn't yet attained the status of being fully human.

The slaves were housed in dormitories in a damp basement. There was an area where slaves were tending a furnace that seemed to be designed to conduct heat upstairs. This room was like a little hell. The slaves were drenched in sweat, working in loincloths that were completely soggy. I felt very fortunate not to be forced to work there.

Croesus had his own room, which was quite roomy —

and held some valuable objects, like some scrolls, a little statue of some god — but also a selection of whips. The rest of the quarters were cramped indeed — each cell held up to a dozen; the beds were raised rectangles of concrete next to which each slave's meagre belongings were held in a small wooden box. I shared a room with the other delicati — the two who had looked at me with such disdain when I'd first stumbled into the triclinium.

My belongings were few, and they had already been deposited by my sleeping space; and the two boys were already searching through them, holding up the mirror. Luckily they had not opened my peculium; I would have to find a good hiding place.

"Your companions in debauchery," Croesus said, sounding very disapproving. "They are called Hyacinth and Hylas."

Hylas was olive-skinned and green-eyed, and smirked at me. Hyacinth, to my amazement, looked as though he could have come from my village. In fact, he immediately spat at me, and hissed in my own language, "Filthy whore."

"You're one to talk!" I said. He merely laughed. Yet it was a relief to hear my own language, even in derision.

"You favorite one now," Hylas said in strangely accented Greek, "but in two years you feeding the ducks in dominus's farm."

Hyacinth said to me, "You've got a tongue. Use it wisely." I did not like the way that sounded at all. The two of them laughed at me.

In my own tongue I asked him, "Are you from a village? Is it near the sea? Do you remember your parents?"

"I should punch you in the face," he answered. "What

village? I'm a fucking prince."

"Me too," I said.

And suddenly we both laughed, and for a moment I thought we might be friends. "Don't speak our language in front of anyone." He made a dismissive gesture to Hylas. "That one doesn't count. He's barely verbal, and anyway he can keep a secret. If they knew we had a secret way of communicating … they'd sell me. Not you! After all, they have you now, the new, improved me, anyway. I'm just about over the hill."

"That's ridiculous," I said. "You … you're beautiful."

"But for how much longer? I'm thinking I'll ask Croesus to take me to have me cut. I'd have a few good years left if I did."

"Cut?"

The two laughed again, but this time it was edgy.

"A few good years," said Hyacinth, "if I survive the operation. Half don't."

Hylas had been going through my things again. "Nice mirror," Hylas said. "Think me keep it."

"Stop being mean," Hyacinth said.

And at that moment, Croesus came back for me.

First I was brought to the master's private bath. Gaius Petronius was already soaking and I realized that we were directly above the hellish basement where slaves had been toiling to stoke the furnace.

I entered the water and was shocked at the heat. No wonder the room beneath us seemed like the depths of infernum itself. My master beckoned. I did not know what to do exactly, so I waded in and began by rubbing his back. He sighed in pleasure. I continued, using my hands to gently massage his arms, as Aristarchos had taught me. Petronius did not demand anything more titillating than that; he merely sat with his eyes closed, occasionally murmuring something in Greek. I wondered whether later on, in the bedchamber, I would be subjected to less savory predations. This kept me on edge. How could he not sense my unease? Or was it simply normal to him, that a slave must always be in fear?

At length, Petronius stood up and went to a marble stool, where he sat, not saying a word, while I wiped him down with a soft cloth, rubbed him down with perfumed olive oil, and scraped him with a strigil. Again, he did not say a word to me.

Then the master took me by the hand and led me to the cubiculum. We were both naked, and my anxiety was now practically at the breaking point. Surely I could not stave off my fate much longer.

I was surprised once more to see that there were others in the room. There were two women on the bed — the same giantesses who had come to prepare me for delivery to this house. They, too, were completely unclad. They shifted position so that Petronius could get between them, but made no move to accommodate me.

"Stand right there," Petronius said. "In front of my bed. I want to look at you while I write my novel."

Then, one of the women, the darker, pulled out a writing tablet and a stylus from under the bed, The other offered him wine in a rhyton of precious, rainbow-fringed glass. All I did was stand there. Two slaves held up a damask veil behind me, and another fanned the veil, not to cool me, but to create a billowing effect.

And my dominus wrote on the tablet, looking at me as

he wrote: *"Dum haec loquimur, puer speciosus, vitibus hederisque reditimus, modo Bromium, intendum Lyaeum Euhiumque confessus …* 'as we were conversing, a gorgeous boy with grapeleaves and ivy in his hair brought grapes in a basket, imitating Bacchus in ecstasy, dreaming, full of wine …'"   He went on in this vein for some time, composing as he wrote.   Now and then he told me to turn around.   "You are the perfect model for my Giton," he said. "I just have to hope your looks can be distilled by my stylus into words.   Turn again, smile a little.   Are you tired? Share some of my wine."

"Who is Giton, domine?" I asked him.

"A slave.   And in my book, a supreme object of desire."

"I thought books were about gods and kings and heroes."

"I have a different vision.   I am creating a book that on occasion talks as ordinary people talk, yet also at times soars like the finest classic poetry — a book that talks about art and literature in the same breath as raunchy sex acts and lust and sweat and gluttony and cupidity and treachery and the worst exemplars of human slime … and the beauty of young love.   A book that dwells as much among slaves as among the gods … but which treats them as human beings and not simply as comic relief as in the comedies of Plautus."

While he said all this, I must add, the two women were alternately performing various acts upon him, including "swallowing the serpent" and "polishing the tail."   Yet Gaius Petronius Arbiter seemed quite bored by it all, having eyes only for me.

"And I am in this book, domine?"

"Be quiet and let me write.   More wine, Euphrosyne."

The slave took a break from her ministrations to ply him with more, and also shuffled over to where I was stiffly standing, and gave me a few sips from the same rhyton.

"Crook your elbow a little … now smile."

I did my best.

My master said, "Others may find you are the spitting image of Poppaea Sabina, most ravishing, most monstrous of women. To me, however, you are precisely Giton, the boy in my story, the boy two young men fight over; a boy who is a slave, yet enslaves all who see him; that's you."

I looked at my master, who was writing intently; there were tablets strewn about the bed and I knew he would have to send them off to be properly transcribed. It was tiring to stand so long; I tried resting my weight on first one foot, then another.

Petronius peered at the tablet, then at me. His eyes were piercing. He saw more than my outside. I think he could see everything I had suffered. I loved him, then, because he seemed to know who I was, and because of all the people I had met this evening, he was the one who did not see me as a mere thing to be owned … ironic, because he did, in fact, own me.

Eventually I could see dawn steal in through the drapes.

Petronius dismissed the attendants, had them gather up the tablets, and told them to take them to the scribe. Then he gestured for me to come to the bed.

This must be the moment, I thought. *My fantasy is over. Now comes reality, ripping into my rear end.*

I lay down meekly. My lord and master turned me so that my back was to him, and hugged me like a doll. "You are soft," he said. He stroked my hair for a while. And he fell into a deep sleep.

I lay wide awake, not daring to hope that my fate in this mansion was not to be painfully violated by the master, but simply to be admired, perhaps even loved, as a favorite toy is loved. It was a better destiny than I had been told to expect, and I wondered how long it would last.

His gentleness and consideration were such that I even felt a little regret that he had not wanted more; I had never wanted to be touched by someone before, but now I felt a little surge of feeling. Was I happy? I do not know, but with so much unhappiness before and after, perhaps I should treasure this memory as a time when I was less victim, and more muse.

And thus it was that he began to snore, making it impossible to sleep. He was deafening — so were my thoughts, racing, wondering whether I had finally reached home.

Touching! You lived happily ever after with a rich, mad poet!

You know I did not. You know that I rose much higher than to be the plaything of a senator.

But you have no titillating tales of the private life of the most famous libertine of our times?

Most famous, perhaps, but not so much of a voluptuary as many others I was fated to encounter. You see, he did not even bother to have sex with me. He saw me as something quite other than a convenient hole to plug.

And thus it was that I lay awake until it was broad daylight, when Croesus entered the room and pulled me off the master's bed.

"You are to serve Lord Otho's breakfast," he said. "Oh, and I am to beat you."

"But the dominus said —"

"You are going to ask me to wake him up to ask whether he has countermanded his order? I will get whipped myself! Better your back than mine. Come quickly. Let's get it over with. I'll hurt you as little as I can get away with, and I won't leave any marks."

XI
Marcus Salvius Otho

Croesus had barely touched me, and to be sure he had used the strap with a very gentle hand, before one of the cleaning slaves came down to tell us that Marcus Salvius Otho was awake.

"Well," Croesus said, untying me from the post, "you can't very well serve breakfast while covered in welts."

I took a tray into the guest cubiculum, where Otho lay sprawled out on a huge couch, one that could easily fit three or even more. Doubtless, this room was designed for an orgy. The murals showed Jupiter in particularly concupiscent aspects. On one wall, he chased Leda, in the guise of a swan, though displaying a remarkably human set of genitalia. In another, he chased the nymph Europa. But the wall directly at the head of the bed showed Jupiter snatching Ganymede from the shores of Troy, with golden Ilium's walls in the background and Mount Ida in the distance, and fluffy clouds overhead.

"Your breakfast, *domine*," I said. On the tray were olives, figs, bread, and a cup of wine. I set it down beside the couch and prepared to leave, but Otho grabbed my slender wrist with a plump hand and pulled me down to the bed.

"When I have breakfast in the home of Petronius," he said, "the slave generally feeds me." The way he was looking me up and down, I did not think he would be content with a few figs. Clearly the servus was being served along with the prandium. Perhaps I could get away with being one of the trimmings, rather than the main course.

It did not seem likely.

"Poppaea," Otho murmured in a husky simulacrum of an erotic sigh.

"I am Sporus," I said softly. Otho slapped me soundly, catching me by surprise so I barked in pain, remembering my position just in time.

"You are whoever I say you are, Poppaea, my Poppaea," said Otho. He pulled me closer and he began — I cannot say it more delicately — to slobber. His breath was odious — morning breath combined with sour wine. I closed my eyes and tried to think of my peculium.

Otho took me into his embrace. I was fainting from the stench.

At that moment, however, there was a rescue ... of sorts.

My ravisher suddenly dropped me. I sank down onto the bed. I couldn't really move much, because I was pinned down by the weight of Otho's thighs.

"Oh," Otho said, "good morning, my darling." He was not speaking to me.

I looked up from and saw, in the doorway ... myself.

I knew who it was because I had already seen myself in that piece of mirror that was one of my only belongings.

Myself, that is, with hair elaborately coiffed, wearing a silken stola embroidered with gold thread, held at the shoulder by a fibula in the shape of a Cupid with little diamonds in its eyes.

The Lady Poppaea Sabina, I presumed.

She stared at me, and I at her.

One of the wealthiest noble ladies in the known world, and me, the lowliest of the low, and we were the proverbial two peas in a pod.

"What monstrous obscenity have you found this time?" said the Lady Poppaea Sabina.

Her voice — strident in rage — was nevertheless sheer music.

Her eyes — flashing with the fury of Jove's thunder — were the most sensuous I had ever seen.

I thought ... *Do I really look like that, too? Am I that beautiful?*

"I can explain," Otho said.

"I am sure you cannot," said the Lady Poppaea, bearing down, her palm raised up as if to deliver a resounding slap.

She sat down at the edge of the bed and motioned for Otho to get off me. I wanted to run away, but I knew that I would have to wait for these high-and-mighty aristocrats to dismiss me.

"I'm perfectly aware that I'm the most desirable trophy wife in all of the empire," Poppaea said. "Yet you've taken it on yourself to get yourself an improved model, I see. With certain ... special attachments, I imagine. And doesn't talk back, either. Entirely compliant ... or made so with a dose of the strap."

She tugged me closer, so my eye was level with hers.

"What's your name, slave? You must be a slave. No freeborn lad who looks like you would willingly lie with my piggy of a husband."

"Oh don't be so tiresome, dear," Otho said. "I just woke up. Sporus, give my wife some figs."

"I'm not being tiresome. You've humiliated me in the worst possible way — denigrating the one thing I can't do anything about — the fact that I don't have a penis." She turned to me. "See it from my point of view, Sporus. All my beauty, my intelligence, my wealth ... and I have to play the devoted Roman matron to this effete fat *thing.*"

"Only in public, darling. In private, you can dally with anyone you wish."

"Externally," said Poppaea. "I'm sure you don't want any bastards planted inside me."

"But we have a way to solve this now, my dear. Don't you see? Sporus is a godsend. I finally have a way to bring myself to —"

Thus it was that I performed my first role in service to Gaius Petronius Arbiter, and it was an ignominious one. First, the Lady Poppaea Sabina disrobed and lay down on the bed. Then I lay next to her, face down, with my buttocks elevated by a cunning arrangement of pillows, to facilitate what Otho was planning.

There was a lot of slobbering. Luckily I did not have to see Otho's face. He squashed my slender body, grunting repulsively. "My love," he said. "My Queen, my Empress, my Goddess."

Poppaea whispered in my ear. "You'd better moan," she said. "It will go faster if he thinks you're reciprocating."

I tried a few half-hearted moaning sounds and Otho

instantly became even more aggressive. I screamed, and it was definitely not from pleasure. But the scream got him into a heightened state of excitement. He started pounding away, and presently worked himself up to near-climax. Then he slid off me, landing right on top of his wife, as I rolled off the cubiculum.

I shook myself, got up, and stared down at the bed where Otho was belaboring Poppaea with a couple of perfunctory thrusts. He was able to discharge into his decidedly bored lady wife. He finished, got up, and ordered me to bring him the wine cup.

It was the strangest lovemaking — if it could be called that — I had ever witnessed, let alone been a party to. "Well," he said, "that was lovely. Did you enjoy it, dear?"

"As much as I enjoy the attentions of one of my dogs," she said.

I pulled on my tunica and helped the Lady Poppaea back into her clothes. An attendant entered the room and began to do her hair. When she was dressed, you could not tell what a strange act she had just participated in.

Marcus Salvius Otho got dressed as well, with the help of some slaves who appeared, it seemed, out of nowhere.

No one cleaned me up, of course. I straightened my tunica and hair as best I could. Otho had not actually penetrated me, but I had thought I was going to get killed, such was the violence of his passion. Yet now, that passion spent, he seemed like a perfectly bland, uninteresting person.

"Well, my dear," he said, "that certainly changes things. I imagine, with this little thing as an incentivizer, I could even father a child on you."

"This little thing, as you put it," said Poppaea, "belongs

to someone else. And after this morning's sorry showing, I doubt the little thing's for sale. You need to realize that they're not just objects, you know. Slaves, I mean. They do scurry off to their masters and tell them everything. By the end of today, Petronius will know a lot more about you than he knew yesterday."

Wild-eyed, Otho looked first at me, then at his wife. "He planned this!" he said.

"In politics," said the Lady Poppaea Sabina, "you figure out the opposition's weak spot. And yours, my dear, is that though you may love your wife, you do not love her vagina."

"I'm only human," said Otho.

Poppaea laughed. She pulled me to me and gave me a kiss on the cheek. "Cheer up, boy," she said. "I may help you fill up your peculium yet. Though I've half a mind to have you whipped, just to wipe that smirk off your face. Do you know how difficult it has been to get my husband to perform his ... ah ... duty?"

To Otho, she said, "Now, sit up straight and behave. We are going to say goodbye to our host now. You've overstayed your welcome by passing out drunk at his symposium. And, heavens, the Emperor wants a private cena with you tonight! He's planning to sing you his new song! You've got at least three hours of hot soak, oiling, scraping, perfuming, and beard-trimming before you can face a vocal recital from Himself the Divinity, Pater Patriae, Pontifex Maximus!"

And with that, she pushed her husband out into the hall.

I followed at a discreet distance and caught Otho remonstrating with my master.

I had caught his eye, so I couldn't slink away. He

beckoned me with a crooked finger.

"You don't look well," Petronius said. "I'm afraid I forgot to cancel your whipping. You should tell Croesus that it is perfectly all right to wake me in the morning on any occasion that I've sentenced you to lashes the day before and forgotten to commute. He will say he wouldn't dare wake me, but insist." I knew that insisting was not my place, and that Croesus had beaten me as lightly as he dared, so I decided it would be best to keep silent.

I bowed my head, preferring, perhaps, that my master not know the true extent of my humiliation that morning — not the beating, but being treated as some kind of surrogate wife. I felt pity for Poppaea, even though I hardly had the right to feel pity for someone so much more privileged than I — but for all that privilege I sensed she was as trapped as I was.

Otho had been trying to interrupt this conversation and he continued, "Name your price, Petronius. You know I'm good for it. Besides, the boy *loves* me! You should have heard him moan!"

You should have seen Poppaea roll her eyes.

Petronius patted me on the head. "It'll take more than money," he said, "to part me from my Giton. I am as devoted to him as he is to me. *Serva me, servabo te,*" he added, and kissed me on the cheek.

"Poets' drivel," Otho said. "Slaves don't really serve anything but their own self-preservation."

"There, there," Petronius said, patting my cheek again, trying to reassure me. "I'm not going to sell you."

Poppaea looked at both of us, then said, with an evil gleam in her eye, "But you *would* consider giving him away, wouldn't you?"

XII
POPPAEA SABINA

The Lady Poppaea was not wrong. Petronius did not sell me, but he did make a deal. A deal he had every right to make, and he did his best to let me have a share in it. A deal I did not like, but which I could hardly refuse, since my master had gone out of his way to see that I would benefit.

I would be sent to the home of Marcus Salvius Otho twice a month, on whichever days that the medicus deemed the Lady Poppaea Sabina would be most likely to conceive. I would have to participate in the strange ritual where I was the object of desire, yet the lady was the object to be inseminated. Otho pledged not to damage me in any way, and to avoid any kind of painful penetration; his enjoyment of my charms was to be purely intercrural. Two guards, hand-picked by Marcus Vinicius, would escort me there and back. I would be returned to the home of my master before dawn.

For this peculiar service, I would collect from the Lord Otho the princely sum of three denarii, of which I would add one to my peculium, and hand over two to Croesus, who would note it all down in the house records.

It did not seem like a bad arrangement. My function was solely as a facilitator. I did not need to have any kind of relationship with "the piggy husband," as the Lady Poppaea called him.

Unfortunately, Otho was never quite able to stick to the no-damage clause. No matter what he had agreed to, I drove him mad, it seemed. The first night I returned to the domus Petronii bleeding and in tears. Maddened by pain and disillusionment, I charged straight into my master's cubiculum and threw myself at him, sobbing. Croesus came right behind me, wielding a strap, but it was too late; I had aroused the one known throughout Rome for sleeping all day and carousing all night.

Croesus immediately prostrated himself abjectly at the foot of the bed. "Master," he said, "I don't know how I let this happen ... I have not dared awaken you in three decades of service ... beat me within an inch of my life, Gaius Petronius, but I beg you, don't sell me!"

My master was barely awake while all this was going on, but he gradually became aware of a whimpering old slave on the floor and a weeping young one in his arms. He looked at Croesus, and then at me, and — thank the gods — he began laughing. It was a throaty laugh, rich and not unkind, and amazingly, he got me laughing, too. But his demeanor grew serious when he saw blood on my tunica.

"This was not my intention," he said.

"I appreciate that you did not want me hurt —"

"Oh, well, there's that, but it's only common sense.

When you borrow a precious object, you don't return it all bloody. If he'd *bought* you, he'd have done what he liked, I suppose. I hope he tipped you."

"He did, *domine*. I received three denarii plus an extra as."

"One miserable as to salve a bleeding arse! I've a mind to charge him for a full replacement. Not that I'd actually replace you, of course."

A strange mixture of genuine concern and complete callousness. That was how it was, to be master and slave. That is how the relationship is. I never delude myself anymore.

Well, you're not a slave anymore. You're an ex-empress, about to be a god.

And death comes to slaves and empresses alike.

But not gods.

Somehow, I don't believe it. Where I come from, the gods are mortal. Oh, they live a very long time, far longer than any human being, and yet there will come a time when they fight the ultimate darkness, and the darkness wins. As it always does.

Where do you come from? You never said.

One barbarian village is much like another. What difference does it make?

It will take some time for your hair to conform to the shape I have designed. If I bore you, I can leave for a while, as I can't go on with your makeup until the hair is firmed up.

Do I have to sit here? Perhaps the guard can take me on a little tour? Where do they keep the lions? I love cats.

Oh, the lions. Come. I will walk with you, and you can tell me more scandalous tales, perhaps over a haunch of Christian.

The Christians! I had a run-in with them, too. But that is much later. For now, the stately homes of two wealthy noblemen were all I had seen of the grandeur of Rome.

I had at least a fortnight before my next session at the house of Otho. I spent the time in improving my languages; I yearned to speak as eloquently as my master, who could leap from vaulting poetry to coarse vulgarity in the confines of one sentence. Latin is a language of incredible precision — Greek, on the other hand, revels in ambiguity and veiled revelations. My speaking improved by leaps and bounds because each night, my master read to me from his novel-in-progress, and the adventures of Encolpius, Ascyltus, and Giton were not just exciting, but lessons in every level of the Latin language, from the exalted to the obscene.

As for my roommates, Hylas and Hyacinth, they calmed down considerably when they realized I wasn't about to deprive them of their jobs. The master held symposia almost every other night, and at those, I was rarely trotted out; Hylas and Hyacinth collected the tips. At normal dinners, with fewer guests, my master made me chief cupbearer and my duties were more like Ganymede in Olympus than a by-the-hour boy in a lupanar. Late into the night, Petronius would read to me, or speak to me, or rather *at* me, about life at court, about the Emperor's wild poetry, and about how he had to neither flatter nor demean, and the fine line he had to walk to keep Himself the Divinity's favor.

At length, the time came for another visit to the house of Otho. As before, two legionaries escorted me and my litter was carried downhill a little way, through winding, irregular streets — it was not far. This time, with the worst to expect already in my mind, I was able to gaze at the scenery.

Unless he is as rich as my master, a Roman lives on the street — he eats, defecates, shops, copulates in dark corners, and strolls over to the public baths to clean up after all of it, through a labyrinth where no streets are marked and where no one gives directions. The litter was not just for comfort, though of course it did protect against the odors of the open gutter and the occasional projectile turd.

One of the most striking aspects of the city streets by day was the sheer color and variety of the graffiti. Sexual boasts, poems praising gladiators, and religious slogans like "fuck the Christians" were on the walls, as well as political advertisements, hopefuls running for quaestor or tribune.

Though I was a slave, the fact that was carried on a litter by a matched team of slaves meant that people assumed I *was* somebody. Later I was to learn that all sorts of slaves are somebodies ... many of them run the empire's finances, shape political actions, and influence the very visions of the great. For now, I pretended to be important. When I stepped into the atrium of Marcus Salvius Otho, my fantasy could continue because my house servants deferred to me, fed me well, and made sure I was bathed and perfumed before being led to my fate.

Knowing what to expect now, I was able to manipulate my buttocks and thighs so that I always managed to avoid being speared on the senatorial member. This actually seemed to inflame him all the more. I felt as though I was being probed by an elephant's trunk. Taking the Lady

Poppaea's advice to heart, I moaned, perhaps more convincingly than the previous time, because Otho's heavings became ever more suffocating.

Meanwhile, the Lady Poppaea Sabina lay languidly, her flesh cool as snow, sipping from a kylix of resinated Lesbian wine.

When the necessary moment came for Otho's *coitus* to become *interruptus*, I swiftly slid off the cushions and allowed the Lord to breach the Lady, who had smoothed the way with a lubricious infusion of olive oil. He came, I think, rather copiously, and immediately began snoring.

"Help me get out from under this lump," said the Lady Poppaea Sabina. I hopped over to her side and helped pull her free. Otho rolled to the edge of the bed, leaving the Lady Poppaea Sabina and I practically on top of each other and, I was embarrassed to discover, rendering me considerably more excited than I had been by her boorish husband.

"Oh!" Poppaea said, giggling. This was the first emotion I'd seen in her all evening. "I didn't realize you were able to actually ... *enjoy* ... it."

"I didn't, either."

"After last time, I supposed you traumatized for life."

"Very nearly, domina."

"I certainly was," she said. "Can you imagine anything more awful than to be me, the most glamorous, most beautiful, richest, cleverest woman in all Rome — being wedded to someone who doesn't even like women?"

"I wouldn't know, my Lady."

"With all that heaving and grunting, I'm as dry as a papyrus in Egypt," she said. "But perhaps *you* could ... no. I'd be taking advantage of a dear friend."

"You can command me anyway you like, domina."

"I mean Petronius, silly. You're just a toy. And yet ... I've often wondered what kind of a lover I would be, if I had a little *phallos* of my own."

Suddenly, the advice of Hyancinth, my compatriot and colleague in depravity, came back to me. "You've got a tongue. Use it wisely."

I did.

How wise it was I do not know, but in mere moments, the Lady Poppaea Sabina was shrieking in ecstasy. "Oh! Oh! Remind me to send Petronius a brace of my cook's legendary stuffed geese!" she murmured in between moans. (As I was otherwise engaged, I was unable to respond.) At length she reached some kind of climax, and as she lay panting, I plied her with another cupful of retsina. She turned to order some attendant, kneeling in a corner, to send along the brace of geese and a jar of figs along with my litter. She then reached into a pouch next to the lectus. "I haven't any change, and I don't suppose you can change an aureus," she said, sighing, tossing me a gold coin. I had never seen one. I tried to refrain from gawking. "You deserve it, for the momentary pleasure you brought an old woman."

"Old!" I cried. "You must be joking, domina."

"Sporus," she said — I remember sitting straight up at the shock that she remembered my name — "I'm seven years older than Piggy, and seven times more intelligent, and at least seven times as rich. I don't *like* my husband. He's not my first, and I promise you, he won't be my last. I have my eye on a much bigger prize."

"Who?" I asked, in all innocence.

"Oh, someone I knew in my childhood as Lucius. Lucius

Domitius Ahenobarbus." She pointed to the gold coin in my hand.

"You mean the Emperor!" I said. Even a lowly slave like me knew by now the birth name of Himself the Divinity, Nero Claudius Caesar Augustus Germanicus, Imperator, Pater Patriae, Pontifex Maximus, and so on so forth. One wouldn't presume to call the Divinity by his human childhood name unless one actually *was* a childhood playmate.

"Perhaps you didn't even think a woman like me could hope to marry the Emperor, who is, after all, already married, and to his stepsister at that, Octavia, the daughter of his uncle, the Emperor Claudius."

"I don't normally think about such things at all. I'm a slave, remember?"

"I know what you're thinking," she said to me. "But I have a plan. And I have an edge."

"An edge?" I asked her.

"A secret weapon. I have you," she said, her eyes sparkling.

XIII
WEDDING-GIFT

I returned to my master's house more confused than ever. I gave the geese to Croesus, who told me that the slaves' quarters would sing my praises for such largesse; when I told him that the Lady Poppaea had meant Petronius to have them, he laughed it off. "We don't share tips with the dominus," he said.

About my other tip, the golden aureus, I was in a panic. I did not dare show it to anyone, because I didn't want people picking through my peculium.

In fact, I trusted my master, who technically owned my peculium anyway, more than any of the slaves of the household. And so I slipped into his bedroom — I knew he would not have awoken — and, after folding my clothes neatly at the foot of the lectulus, I slid in beside him, meaning to ask him first thing when he woke up.

It was past noon when I felt him stir; he had hugged me close to him, as a child might a doll; he had a unique scent, part perfumed olive oil part old wine, that filled my nostrils. I opened my eyes to see him looking down at me.

"My Giton," he said. "I gave no command for you to be sent to my bed after coming back from Otho's house." He stroked my hair and added, "But at least you're not in tears, and you haven't left any bloodstains on my bed."

I told Petronius that the Lady Poppaea had given me a whole aureus, since she had no change. "Should I give it to you, *domine?* It doesn't seem right for a slave to carry gold on him."

Petronius laughed. "Our Supreme Lord and God, Himself the Divinity, once bet four hundred thousand sesterces on a single roll of dice! That's four thousand of those things. Once the Late and Unlamented Caligula spent ten million sesterces on a banquet. You're going to be rich long before you're free. If I ever even agree to your manumission; why would I ever let such a lovely thing go?"

"You will soon enough, domine, when I start to lose my looks. Everyone says so."

"Your looks will live on in my book, Sporus," said Petronius Arbiter.

I did not tell him about the Lady Poppaea's imperial ambitions. Perhaps I should have. He might have warned me off, or protected me a little better; then again, in the end he could not even protect himself.

I'm getting a bit impatient. We all want to hear about Nero. After all, ever since the day they decreed damnatio memoriae *upon him, we no longer hear all those wild stories of indulgence and decadence. In fact, we can't get anyone to talk about Himself the Late Divinity at all. And they're chipping his name off all the big monuments.*

Why do you think *I'll* tell you anything?

Because you're going to die anyway.

True enough. I will tell you one thing. There has been a

massive campaign to blacken Nero's name, though less
than a year has passed. But I was with him. I was the one
to whom he whispered his last words. Not some senator
or trusted guard, and certainly not his mistress Actë,
though she has since dined out on many a scandalous
story.

Remember, too, that there was never an official
senatorial decree of *damnatio.* No one is going to be
arrested for talking about him. Allowing a kind word once
in a while is not going to lead to being strung up on a
cross.

He may have murdered his mother and kicked his wife
to death, but remember that he lowered your taxes.

I don't pay taxes, silly. I'm a slave.

Fair enough.

He was a monster to some. Indeed, he had my balls cut
off. And yet, he loved me.

As much as a god is capable of love.

And yet my first sight of the most powerful man in the
universe was not edifying. It seemed that my master was
invited — not too willingly — to a banquet at the home of
a man named Tigellinus. Now this Tigellinus was the
commander of the Praetorian Guard, I heard. He had
power. Marcus Vinicius had dropped his name a few
times. This banquet was going to be attended by Rome's
elite.

"I hate these affairs," Petronius said. "I'm told there will
be a wedding. In that case, perhaps lavish gifts will be
distributed to the guests. Your duty will be to wait in an
anteroom with the other slaves and, should I receive such a
gift, to carry it out to my litter. It won't do to carry such a

thing myself ... I'll need a pretty young thing to do the carrying. I've got appearances to uphold."

"Couldn't one of the other boys do it, domine?"

"Of course, Sporus, but I am fond of your company! I shall get out of this hideous obligation all the more quickly, if I know you're going to be accompanying me in the litter going home. I'll need to unload a year's worth of scandalous gossip, and you're too loyal, too discreet, and too innocent, to go selling information."

"I wouldn't know who to sell it to, master."

I had a bad feeling, but a slave has no say. It was a long journey; Tigellinus's house was all the way on the Palatine, and mostly uphill for the litter-bearers. I could not really believe that my master would bring me along just to carry something that he might not even receive. Or that he was merely fond of my company.

But a slave has no say.

When we finally reached this home, which was by no means the palatial wonder I expected, we could see that it was surrounded by guards, and that all sorts of swords, daggers, and even little knives that could barely peel an apple had been temporarily held on a table just inside the entrance. Someone was being very strict about security.

We slaves were inspected very thoroughly and indeed somewhat roughly handled. A burly centurion even looked up the back of my tunica. Then I and the litter-bearers were sent to a large waiting room with stairs that seemed to lead down to a dungeon-like slaves' quarters, with a soldier guarding the door.

My master joined a stream of guests and I was able to look at my new surroundings. This room was a madhouse. Petronius would never abide a mess like this, and litter-bearers usually waited in the street anyway; they were probably glad of being inside, for it promised to be a long banquet indeed.

There were teams of litter-bearers, most of them matched — they were all Numidians, all Germans, all Nubians, all Britons, all superb physical specimens, well-oiled and not wearing much clothing, as if their owners wanted to show off every inch of what they possessed. Other teams were clearly thrown together with little care: paunchy with scrawny, hairy with bald, and uncoordinated dress; these probably had owners more interested in getting where they were going than any kind of ostentatious display, or perhaps really important people who preferred to travel anonymously.

There were slaves like me, basically there to ornament their owner, to carry things, or perhaps to provide a quick orgasm on the long ride back. I sat for a while, listening to the chatter; I had not heard so many languages in one room since being penned up in Ostia.

I didn't want to draw attention, so I squeezed myself into a corner, put my head between my knees, and waited.

At length, a man loomed over me and spoke to me in my native language. "Don't often see one of *us*," he said.

I didn't answer.

"It's all right, boy," he said. "When we talk, no one will listen. That's because where we come from, the Empire does not really extend; only the pirates do. I would love to hear news of our country. I have been here … a long time."

I looked at him. He was one of the unmatched litter-bearers. He must have noticed my curiosity, because he started to explain. "My master is a Stoic," he said. "He's not into ostentation."

"What's a Stoic?"

"It's a philosophy, a way of life. Personally, it is not that different from what I believe. I am a Christianos."

"What's that?"

"I would love to tell you, but this is not the time."

We were interrupted by sounds from the basement. Someone was being whipped, and was screaming. The cries were more animal than human; I could not even tell if it was a man or a woman.

"This is a strict house," said my compatriot. "Someone is always being whipped down there. You, on the other hand, you don't carry yourself like someone who is afraid of the flagellum."

"I've had a few beatings," I said, though I was almost embarrassed to admit how few.

"My master has been to your house," he said. "I saw you once, in the distance. My master is the tragic poet, Seneca. He once wrote, *Divitae bonum non sunt.*" Which I could interpret now as something like, "Material things aren't the one good thing in life."

He saw me before? It must have been at the symposium then, the day I first laid eyes on Gaius Petronius Arbiter. "If you need to speak our language," he said, "find a pretext to send a message to the house of Seneca, or look for me when my master visits yours ... I think he plans to come on the Kalends, for a poetry reading. My name is Viridian. Well, my real name is ..." And he spoke a name in my native tongue.

I wasn't interested. I wanted my past walled off. I was subsisting in a strange half-world, learning every day, as a baby learns. I did not want to be shackled by the past when I was already chained up in the present. I tried to brush off this conversation and asked him where I could relieve myself.

"They are strict in this house," Viridian said. "There is an amphora down the hall to the left, on this side of the peristyle. This house does its own laundry, so they need to collect every drop of piss they can. Ten lashes if you go in the bushes."

"They beat other people's slaves?"

"No master is going to quibble about ten," he said.

He pointed the way and whispered something to the guard, who motioned me through. But, as seemed to always happen to me when I went for a piss in an unfamiliar mansion, I made a wrong turn, and I found myself standing in a doorway.

What I saw was so strange I could not look away. I was looking into a triclinium, but it was far grander than the one in Petronius's house. Indeed, where I was standing was a black marble pedestal in the shape of a Corinthian column, on which was perched a more-than-life-sized bust of the Emperor. I knew him from the coins. On the aureus, the portrait was particularly clear.

No one could see me, in the shadow of a column. But I saw —

First, a lectus had been laid out in the center of the room. Around it, guests on couches, decked out in fine fabrics and glittering baubles, had abandoned their dinner to stare at the couch. I recognized the Lady Poppaea, and Marcus Salvius Otho and even my friend, Marcus Vinicius … and everyone else must have been just as lofty as those patricians. A rhythmic music on drums, double-flutes and finger cymbals was rousing the guests to fever pitch as they observed the goings-on.

A woman in a *tunica recta* — dressed as a bride, that is — crouched on her hands and knees. The *zona*, which should have symbolized virginity in such wedding garments, was not double-knotted but loosened, and the back of her tunica was hitched up, exposing her buttocks. Rearing above her was a sweat-drenched, bearded man wearing a golden wreath and nothing else, and he was pumping away at the woman's posterior as the guests chanting *Feliciter! Feliciter!* and quaffed wine from oversized cups.

The woman was shrieking and moaning in a what was almost a parody of erotic exaltation. The guests were cheering and calling out the groom's name now: *Pythagoras! Pythagoras!*

As I stared, the exhibition mounted to a climax and the bride was clawing at the air — and then, a lusty scream escaped her throat and a spasm shook her — and then her wig flew into the air and right onto my face!

Panicking, I looked up. As the wig slid down to the floor, the bride looked straight at me. We saw each other clearly. And, as I looked away — looked at *anything* rather than the egregious spectacle in front of me — my gaze fell on the bust I stood next, and I realized who that woman was.

And the woman cried out: "Lo! The God Hymen himself comes down from heaven to bless this sacrament!"

At that moment, there was a hand on my shoulder. I was about to scream, but another hand closed my mouth and yanked me away. It was Viridian.

He marched me down the peristyle. I said, "But I haven't pissed yet — and I'm about to burst!"

"Too late. Your master sent for you."

And there he was, Gaius Petronius Arbiter. In a splendid

toga and wreath, displaying not the slightest dishevelment. He was furious. I had barely registered his expression of rage when I felt the sting of his slap on my cheek. "Domine!" I cried out.

I knew I deserved the slap, and much more. For a slave is property; when a slave misbehaves, it's the owner who looks the fool.

But Petronius's anger dissipated quickly. "I tire of the banquet, and I have slipped away," he said. "There are at least twenty more courses … post-coital sweetmeats, I suppose. They will all be in a stupor by dawn; no one will miss me. Carry this."

He threw a bag at me. It was small, but heavy. I didn't doubt that whatever it contained must be solid gold. I peeked in the bag and it appeared to be a gold statuette of the God Hymen — such irony!

Petronius pushed me toward the door, stopping for a moment to pick up his dagger from the attendant.

"Master —" I began, as the litter began to move bumpily downhill, led by a link-boy with a torch.

"I was going to tell you the gossip," Petronius said, "but it looks like you've seen it for yourself. And lived it, as well!"

"Domine," I said, "I was only trying to find the pee-bucket for the house laundry."

"And I suppose you're going to go all over my nice litter now," Petronius said.

"*Domine* —" I braced for another slap.

"My slaves piss and shit where they please, it seems." He called out to the head bearer. "Toilet break!" The litter came to a stop at a steep angle. My master parted the curtain slightly and said, "Do your business, boy."

I lifted my tunica and urinated into the night … splash, trickle, plink, straight into the gutter … the only sound on the Palatine, in the deep darkness.

"A ritual asperging from the God of Marriage himself!" Petronius said. "Shall I quote Catullus? *Hymen O Hymenaee, Hymen ades O Hymenaee!"*

"You mock me, my Lord." I put my mentula back in my tunica. We moved off. "And yet, I would really love to know —"

"I'm sure you would!"

"The bride tonight — was that really the Emperor?"

"The gods may assume any form," said my master. I did not realize he was joking. So he laughed heartily, slapping me on the shoulder a few times. His humor was infectious and I laughed too.

Then he stopped, and I stopped, too. I could sense his eyes on me in the dark.

"My Giton," he said. "You will speak of this to no one. *On pain of death!* Did the Emperor get a good look at your face?"

"I … think so, domine."

"Then you are doomed," said Gaius Petronius Arbiter.

XIV

DORMOUSE

Doom, however, was not imminent.

In fact, the next day was much like any other, a routine day. As were several days to follow. Days of learning how to comport myself, how to modulate my voice to land precisely the spoken tones that Roman aristocrats found delicate and seductive, of learning which wines went with which foods, of tasting for the first time strange sea creatures, and desserts cooled with mountain snow.

Days of becoming more proficient in the languages of the world into which I had been thrust. Of the subtleties of Greek, whose different genres of literature are written in distinct dialects.

Nights I often fell asleep in the bed of my master, not realizing in my innocence that it was a presumptuous overreach for a slave to do so without being commanded. But it was only because, drunk on Greek poetry and wine, I did not have the strength to crawl back to the tiny cell I shared with Hylas and Hyacinth.

To tell the truth, sleeping with Hylas and Hyacinth was

not as bad as it seemed it would be, the first night I was there. Hylas, who was not very verbal in *any* language, was a boy who endured life rather than living it. Hyacinth, on the other hand, always wanted to talk.

Late at night, he often waited up for me.

One night, with Hylas snoring very loudly, he said, "I'd like to go speak to our gods. Will you come?"

I said, "They won't listen."

"They *have* to, Sporus. I've grown a whole digitus just in the time you've been here. I need help."

We stole into the atrium in the moonlight wearing only *subligacula*, for the night was warm. Slaves should not really be seen unless called for, but tonight was not a party night and there was no one there. It was a simple garden, with an archaic herm at one end mounted on a column, and a statue of Cupid ... a real antique, for the paint had worn almost completely white, and the youth stood stiffly, in an angular way, not like the smooth natural curves of a modern statue.

"Which will it be?" I whispered. "The battered herm or the weathered God of Love?" For neither of those gods was worshipped in our villages. Rather it was trees, rocks, and streams ... nothing that looked human.

But gods, everywhere in the world, are alike in one thing. If you're going to bargain with them, you have to pay in pain. If not your own, then some other creature's.

Hyacinth, of course, didn't have power over other creatures, in order to make them suffer on his behalf. I thought he would do something symbolic, like hack off a hank of hair, or cut himself and drip some blood onto the hungry earth. Instead, he pulled a dormouse from his pouch.

It was fat, having already spent the last month running around aimlessly in its fattening jar.

"The master will have your hide," I said, whistling. "Cook's been fattening them up for the Emperor."

"I'm desperate," he said. The moon lit up his pale features. Sweat clung to his face ... or were they tears?

He held up the dormouse in clasped hands. He said, "Moon, you see everything that happens in the night. Murder, stealth, thievery, sickness, death ... and love. They call me Hyacinth here, but I have a secret name too, which I will only utter in your presence." He then whispered something. That was the custom in our village, too, keeping one's true name secret.

Hyacinth then said, "I beg you, by the sacred moonlight that bathes me, do not let me grow another digitus. Don't let my voice drop to the bark of a grown man. Keep me on the cusp of manhood. Or I'll have nothing left. I'll end up in the fields, or in the mines, or chained to an oar."

"Don't be ridiculous," I mumbled. "Our master's not like that."

"Yes, but he's walking a fine line," Hyacinth grated. "This game of simultaneously flattering and ridiculing the Emperor ... he's going to make a false step, and we'll all be on the auction block." He held up the dormouse and, putting both hands around its fat neck, prepared to throttle it. "I offer you the life of this dormouse," he said, "in exchange for your favor."

But this drama was to no avail. The creature squirmed and slipped from Hyacinth's grasp. It ran into the grass and Hyacinth got down on his hands and knees to catch it, but it scampered away. "Help me grab it!" he said. But for a moment the sight of this desperate boy pursuing a rodent in the grass, in the moonlight, in only a loincloth, was outlandishly comical. I almost laughed, but I caught myself in time.

In a moment, I was on the ground too, scrabbling after this surprisingly nimble dormouse. My loincloth snagged on the pedestal of the herm. Somehow Hyacinth's, too, had got lost in the grass. I knew we'd never escape the whip no matter what and it was in desperation that drove us ... "Fuck you. You *made* me lose the mouse," Hyacinth said, and punched me. I punched back. In moments we were wrestling. And then we *were* laughing. And weeping. The absurdity. The life-and-death ridiculousness of our situation. But suddenly —

"Look! Let go! There it is!"

I pointed. The dormouse had reached the edge of the atrium. It was about to spring up onto the walkway. Hyacinth stretched out his hand and dived for it.

Instead, the dormouse ran right into someone else's hands. We both looked up. Hylas held a flaming torch above us, and kneeling on the ground, having deftly caught the mouse, was Croesus, who, holding it gingerly by the tail, dropped it back into its fattening-jar.

"Downstairs, this very second," he said. I had never heard so much menace uttered so softly. "Both of you. Don't forget to gather up your undergarments. Sporus, your *subligaculum* is wrapped around the herm." I was close to pissing myself. "Hylas, bring a whip. A real one."

We stood in Croesus's chamber. We had not even had time to get dressed. Croesus had in his hand not one of the rods he used for administering light punishments, but something that could rip off skin with a single swipe.

In one corner, Hylas was still holding the torch. He wasn't even in trouble, but he was shaking.

"I'm in a very awkward position," Croesus said. "Stealing from the master is bad enough, but these mice were being fattened for Himself the Divinity, who likes to show up at the most inconvenient of times. Theoretically, this isn't just a flogging. You ought to be crucified."

The punishment seemed so extreme as to be unimaginable. My mind went blank, because it was better not to think at all than to contemplate that kind of death.

"Kill me if you like," Hyacinth said tonelessly. "I haven't got a life left anyway. But don't hurt Sporus. He was just keeping me company. And the dominus likes him. *Loves* him."

"The dominus," said Croesus, "had a favorite vase once. It was an original by Polygnotos, not a copy. It showed a beautiful young man making love to an Athenian hetaira. It was four hundred years old. It was the most beautiful thing in this house. The dominus *loved* it. Just as he loves you, Sporus. This did not prevent the master from smashing it to bits one evening in a fit of rage. The next day, he wept over it. But the vase was still smashed. You, Sporus, are beautiful, but it is not the eternal beauty of an ancient Greek vase."

And now, I was truly terrified. I said, "Croesus, I am innocent and if I die from this, it will be a misfortune but, as you say, soon forgotten. But Hyacinth ... he stole the dormouse because he wanted to make a worthy sacrifice to our moon-god ... because he was afraid of losing his looks, afraid of no longer being able to please Petronius. Honestly, his motives were pure. Just one rodent in exchange for being able to give another year or two of pleasure to this household. Surely he should not die for loving his master too much!"

Croesus studied me for a long time. He fiddled with the whip. I have said that I almost pissed myself. I am ashamed to say that in that moment, I actually did.

And Croesus began laughing. "You came up with that entire argument?" he said. "Not even in your native language? You could be a Cicero come back from the dead, if you could only conjugate a few more verbs properly! Wait till I tell the dominus!"

"You're not *going* to tell the dominus," I said. "Remember? Or else ... him and me ... *crucifixi!*"

It is to this incident, perhaps, that I owe my reputation for being able to talk my way out of things.

And yet, here you are. You didn't talk your way out of this.

No, I did not. How much longer until my farewell performance?

Still time to tell more dirty secrets. But don't speak of slaves; it's vulgar. Speak of Emperors and Gods.

But you're a slave yourself.

Yes. I want to know of other worlds, other strata of our world. I want to dream. I want fantasies.

Is that why you work in the Circus?

I work here because my master is Editor of these games. How would I get to choose where I work?

But you *can* choose your dreams.

Yes.

It was now extremely late, close to the time of *gallicinium*. Soon it would be light. I stood there, my legs wet from my terror. Hyacinth was frozen like a statue, and Croesus was still laughing. Eventually, Hylas laughed too, though whether it was because he saw the humor, or because he thought he would be promoted to chief delicatus, I am not certain.

"Assuming that this does not go beyond this room," Croesus said at last, "what is it, Hyacinth, that you want?"

"I want to be castrated," he said.

I gasped.

"Sporus, wipe yourself off. What a waste of perfectly good piss. We have a lot of laundry in this house!" I nodded, looked for a cloth. "Now, Hyacinth, why on Earth would you want that? You might not even survive the operation. And this is Rome, you know. We're not in some barbaric oriental kingdom like Parthia. We don't just keep eunuchs around just for the fun of it."

"I want to prolong ... what I am. If I lose it, I'll just end up scrubbing toilets. Or worse."

"There is nothing sadder than an ageing eunuch," Croesus said

"I'll die young," he said.

At that moment, there was commotion upstairs. One of the women came rushing down the stairs. "Alert!" she cried. "The Emperor! No more than half an hour. A runner came to warn us."

"By the Gods! He must not have slept yet," Croesus said. "Hyacinth, Hylas, get washed and perfumed. The girls will take longer, so rouse a few *now*. The new one from Nubia. He likes a touch of ebony. And a German. You, Hyacinth," he said, glaring, "are fortunate we caught that dormouse."

The boys went off to get ready. I hadn't received any orders so I followed Croesus into the anteroom, where the entire household was gathered. Croesus was barking orders as though he were running the military. Fresh garum from the cellar. The basting-honey for the mice. Slaves to stand in attendance in the hall. Fresh lamps in the triclinium. Tallow candles, braziers, torches set into brackets; it would almost be like daylight. But hadn't Croesus forgotten something?

"I had better wake the dominus," I said softly.

"No," Croesus said. "You had better not."

"But I'm the only one who can."

"Not this time, child," Croesus said. "I have received very specific orders about what to do with you, should the Emperor make a surprise visit. You are not to show your face. You are not to make a sound. You are not even to breathe. On no account is Himself the Divinity to know that you even exist. Otherwise — let me make this clear — otherwise, it is *I* who will be whipped. To death."

XV

DIVINITAS

My curiosity has always been my bane.

Everyone has always presumed to control me by fear, but curiosity always gets the better of me; for what happened next I had only myself to blame.

I was not locked up in my cell. Croesus had not seen fit to chain me. I saw all the household slaves go upstairs, hastening to dust and burnish and polish in the minutes before the Emperor would arrive.

I sat on the floor pondering the imponderable: *Why?* Why was I doomed because Himself the Emperor had caught sight of me? Hadn't he mistaken me for the God Hymen? What had the Lady Poppaea Sabina called me — her secret weapon?

What could be the harm of observing from a distance?

It was foolish of me. In the past months I had been lulled into believing that my life was somehow charmed — despite my lowly condition. In spite of having barely escaped the lash on many occasions, it seems I couldn't help myself. And so, after giving a little time so that the entire household would being making their obeisance to the Emperor, finding myself completely alone in the slaves' quarters, I decided to slip up to the atrium, trusting that no one would notice me. Which they did not.

Himself the Divinity was holding court in the atrium, seated on a golden throne which he must have brought with him, and the entire household was in attendance — on their faces, on the ground. It was, as I have said, not yet dawn. Some slaves held torches aloft, but they were intended to illuminate personages of importance, not some sneaky child. I had emerged right behind the throne.

There was a large wooden chest, with the lid open, right behind the Emperor. I thought I could crouch behind it, but I heard soldiers' caligae somewhere behind and in a slight panic, I crawled into the box. A guard did walk past. And slammed the lid shut before he went on his way.

The smell inside the box was ... well, if could multiply tenfold the stench of cats about to mate ... but I was trapped. To my amazement, the chest I was trapped in had breathing holes, which afforded a perfect view of what was happening in the atrium. I was not too pleased to see what must have been the previous occupant of the box. It was like a cat, but bigger. Like a leopard, but more sleek. It had a collar with a silver chain which was being held by hands that I knew well ... the hands of the Lady Poppaea Sabina.

"It is called a cheetah," she was telling my master, all the while idly stroking the animal, which was alternately growling and baring its teeth. "Isn't it just darling! I rescued him from the Circus. So kind of Himself to let me keep it."

She and Petronius were sitting on either side of the Emperor, and although the entire household were present, my master and the Lady Poppaea were the only people aside from Himself who mattered.

Prostrating before the Emperor was not something one did automatically, but it had recently become the fashion to require it, at least for members of the lower classes. My tutor once told me that although Emperors are deified after they die, since Caligula, they've come to enjoy this kind of obsequy even before being officially declared Gods by the senate. It did seem to be overdoing it, and presently even the Emperor became a bit irritated at looking at a sea of backs. He said to Petronius, "They don't have to worship all the time, you know. We're en famille here."

"I'm sorry, Divinitas," said my dominus. "I rather thought you'd enjoy the novelty of having your inner godlike nature recognized outwardly."

"Ah," said Nero, "it's true that you alone of my friends appreciates me."

"Divinitas, we all do."

"When you say *we,* my dear Petronius," said the Emperor, "you assume that I have more than one friend."

"And do you not, Divinitas?"

"I'm your friend too," Poppaea said softly.

"Get rid of the attendants," said Nero. "Poppaea and I wish to speak to you of ... delicate matters."

Petronius clapped his hands. The slaves all left the atrium.

Now, as Himself was not in the throes of carnal congress, I managed to get a clearer view than last time. He was young, and did not have the jowls and chin he later acquired. I must say that he was at that time an attractive man, and not just because he possessed unlimited power. He also had a beautiful speaking voice, speaking Greek in a formal, archaic way, modulating the tones so that each utterance was like a melisma in an endless melody.

Those who now think him a monster will not admit it, but he had charisma.

"You plan to try out a new poem on me?" Petronius said, waving away the household.

"Later. Later. No, no, I want to discuss ... marriage."

"But Divinitas, you already have a wife ... not to mention a species of husband."

"Oh, Pythagoras ... that was just a whim, really. He knows it. He was just indulging me. Mad, really, that party at Tigellinus's. We were all drunk. I should divorce the man, really, but that would give too much validation to the wedding."

"Divinitas," Petronius said, "how is your Trojan Ode coming?"

"We won't rush the muse." Himself looked at Poppaea, waved a languid hand. "Poppaea ... state secrets."

The Lady Poppaea took the cheetah's leash. "I'll take a stroll and frighten the slaves a bit, then," she said.

When she was out of earshot, Himself said to my master, "I'm going to marry her, you know." He picked up a dormouse by the tail and started sucking the honey sauce, wiping his lips with a fold of his purple garment, which alone was worth the price of a modest mansion.

"Marriage? Is that your state secret, Divinitas?"

I saw the Emperor's face in the torchlight. What glittered in his eyes was a thing I could never possess — certainty. Which came with absolute power.

I could see that Petronius felt an obligation now to "fix"

things. "That will be a scandal, Caesar," he said, "though as a God, you must know that Gods have a tendency not to mind scandals."

"Take care, Gaius." The menace was muted, but I could see my master adjust his thinking quickly. "You're my arbiter of taste, Petronius! Tell me this is not madness! I'm besotted, bewitched ... bewilderingly so. For as you know, I normally have perfect control of my emotions, and do nothing on a whim."

"Indeed not, Divinity," Petronius said. "You are quite rational, for a God. Though we mortals sometimes cannot perceive it ... that is our fault alone."

There he was, steering the ship of his wit so carefully between the Scylla of flattery and the Charybdis of condescension!

"But ... Divinity ... she *is* married. And more to the point, so are you, and the Lady Octavia is a direct link to the founder of this Julio-Claudian Dynasty ... dare I say it, more direct than your Divine Mother's." The Emperor's face clouded, but only briefly.

"I suppose I could have them killed," Nero said.

"As a God, you can do anything you like," said my dominus, "but ... the Lady Octavia is popular."

"I'll just send them away, then. Out of sight, out of mind."

"The Lady Poppaea is, indeed, beautiful. But she has already been your mistress for some time, has she not?"

"Oh, but she's more than that. Look at her, walking through the garden with that wild animal. It eats out of her hand! If anyone can tame me, and I am not willingly tamed ... it's her. She *must* become Empress."

"Then you will do whatever you think fit, Divinitas, to

achieve that will. For you *are* Rome, and Rome always gets what she wants."

"Very well," said the Emperor. He gestured at the shadows.

I was getting more and more uncomfortable in the confined space of this box, and I needed to get out soon — or I would be sharing the space with a vicious feline. I tried not to breathe. The Lady Poppaea's cheetah become excited suddenly, and practically dragged her toward the box. I could smell the animal's foul breath as he sniffed at the breathing hole. I'm sure he saw me as a meal. "Calm down, Hercules!" said the Lady Poppaea. "If you don't behave, I'll have to put you back in the box."

Luckily the animal listened to its mistress and, whimpering, returned to heel. "Your private business discussed?" she said to the Emperor ... and, I realized now, her lover.

"One other thing," the Emperor said. "You've recently acquired a most delightful puer delicatus, I hear. I want him."

My world fell apart. Petronius's house, if not Olympus, was as close to heaven as a slave could hope for in the real world. I may have gasped. No one noticed. Maybe they just thought it was one of the night-creatures in the garden.

"Of course, Divinity," Petronius said. "All I possess is yours."

He clapped his hands and Croesus appeared as if by magic. "Bring Hylas and Hyacinth," he said. The two boys emerged ... also as if by magic.

"Don't be afraid, boys," Petronius said. "The Emperor won't bite."

"Well," the Emperor chuckled, "not right now, at any

rate."

Poppaea said, "He has been known to tie people up, dress up as a wild animal, and voraciously attack their genitals, after which they are dispatched by the Praetorian Guard."

The two boys looked horrified. There was, of course, no escape.

"Neither is the one I told you about, dearest," Lady Poppaea said. "They don't look a bit like me."

"Come forward." Anxiously, Nero got out of his throne and approached them before they could approach him. He held up a torch himself, peering into their faces. "Not in the slightest," he said. "Be off with you."

The boys scampered away. Relieved, I am sure.

"I'm not making it up," said the Lady Poppaea.

"What are you hiding from me, Gaius Petronius Arbiter?" the Emperor said, stroking my master's cheek, as a cat toys with a mouse.

"Some of the boys have been sent on to Antium," he said. "We're taking the household there ahead of the heat and stench of summer."

The Emperor nodded. "Wise as always, Gaius," he said. "I'll come and collect him when we move the court. Though, to be honest, I might have completely forgotten the whole thing by then."

"The whims of the Gods are truly inscrutable, Divinitas," said Petronius.

"I will keep you guessing. Poppaea, come."

The Emperor called for his litter. But Poppaea tarried a moment. "I shall follow," she said. "I have a few secrets of my own to talk over with Petronius."

The Emperor left the atrium. All sorts of slaves, soldiers,

a pair of bucina-players and a drummer, emerged from the shadows, and prepared to escort him back. Two burly Nubians carried out the throne. My master was alone with Poppaea and a cheetah.

Poppaea said to Petronius. "So, you've hidden him. It's a pity. I so wanted to have him as a little bit of spice in our ... nightly entertainments. Spice, you know, is what he craves the most, and the spicier the better. Having little Sporus on hand is the most convenient way for the beautiful and extremely feminine Poppaea Sabina to grow the occasional penis. But I'll come up with other diversions. Well done knowing we were on our way. Spies in the palace?"

My master did not answer.

"It doesn't matter," she said. "Octavia will be disposed of, and so will Otho. Without any fuss. No need to stoop to assassinations; just, as the Divinitas said ... out of sight, out of mind. But you'll do your part, of course. Your honeyed tongue can make black look like white, and you'll mollify any critics. You'll keep the politicians in line. And most importantly, the poets. They'll all follow your lead."

"I see."

"But I need you to promise to do your part. You'll be richly rewarded, I'm sure. Imagine, if you will, scenes from the Satyricon painted on the walls of Nero's new palace ... or Trimalchio's banquet immortalized as a comic drama!"

"My work is its own reward, Lady Poppaea, and I'm wealthy enough; apart from a predilection for late nights of drinking and whoring, I follow more the Stoic philosophy."

"Well ... we understand each other, I think ... as two snakes, circling the same mouse."

And they both laughed.

Poppaea said, "Oh! Hercules! You sweet little pussywussy, it's time for you to get back in your little boxie-woxie!"

I was doomed. I could smell the cheetah and now I could feel his paws on the lid. Which Poppaea opened. My life was over.

Poppaea and my dominus were looming above the box. I was an insignificant boy in a loincloth, shrinking away from a blow ... or a mauling.

"Antium!" Poppaea was cackling.

My master shrugged. "That is the most troublesome boy I have ever owned," he said. "I've half a mind to put you in with the cat and lock the chest."

"Beat me, domine," I said, "Beat me as hard as you want, but don't give me away. I want to be part of your household forever. The pirates took away everything, my family, my whole world. You're my world now." I could feel hot tears spurting. "I love you, domine, I really do," I said. I put my arms around his knees and held him tight, trying to manipulate my grovelling so that my lips were hovering over just the right spot.

"This is rich," said the Lady Poppaea Sabina. "Don't beat him, he's far too amusing. And whatever you do, don't cut off his tongue. Though I imagine you already know that."

"Oh, I do," said Gaius Petronius Arbiter. Though in truth, he had never forced anything into my mouth that I had not accepted with gratitude and willingness.

"Keep him for now," Poppaea said. "You'll need a good wedding gift."

XVI
Claudia Octavia

So you staved off the Emperor's attentions for a while.

Not for ever, as is well known. But it is true that he was always easily distracted. I would not lay eyes on him again until my master took me to Antium, to escape the oppressive humidity of the Roman summer.

From one kind of humidity to a worse, I suppose!

You could say that.

And were you, in fact, the wedding gift for the Coronation of the Lady Poppaea?

Let me tell it at my own pace.

I will. Though I'm not the one with only a day to live.

Though we had managed to keep the Emperor's hands off me, at least for a while, the same could not be said for the plump and sweaty hands of Marcus Salvius Otho, which roved more aggressively with every visit. Fortunately, I was able to figure out how to drive him to such heights of lust that he would tire out quickly and fall into a deep sleep.

Each session with Otho would be followed by a less frenetic time with the Lady Poppaea, whose company I was beginning to enjoy, in a strange way. The one characteristic they shared, of course, was complete selfishness with regard to pleasure; I was there to facilitate their desires, not to fulfill any of my own; for what needs could a slave possibly have, except the need to eat, sleep, and avoid the lash?

But while Otho grabbed me and gripped me and groped me, groaning and moaning, I was just a thing to him, a thing that conveniently resembled his wife yet possessed the appendages he craved. The Lady Poppaea was different. Although she was equally inconsiderate to me when pleasuring herself, once she was satisfied, she talked to me, even confided in me.

She told me so much that I could have held her destiny in my hands, except that I knew a slave's word cannot be held true in a court of law without having been tortured to extract that word. The Romans used us for everything, even, in their way, loved us, but they feared us, too.

And one morning, after a night of such confidences, Poppaea announced she was taking me to visit someone. It pleased her to have me sit with her as she enjoyed some bread, wine, and olives, with Hercules the cheetah at her feet. Occasionally she would toss me an olive and have me catch it in my mouth. My hands were not free since it took all my strength to grip the chain that kept Hercules at heel. She would also toss the animal a hunk of flesh from time to time — a tidbit of mouse or a leftover peacock's brain. I was a pet animal, like Hercules, but could perform many more tricks.

I have to admit that Hercules was growing on me. He

actually let him pet him and he would nuzzle up, rub up against my leg … once I was convinced he would not start nibbling or gnawing, I was content to let him, though he was a bit rank, as wild animals tend to be.

"Oh don't worry, Sporus," the Lady Poppaea said. "I've already sent word to your master and he has said you need not be home until supper. And you're so good with Hercules! I don't trust anyone else to hold his leash. You will relish this visit, I am sure. It's someone I talk about all the time."

"Who, domina?" I said.

"I'll tell you later."

"Why, domina, are we visiting this person?"

"To gloat."

Our destination was the Oppian Hill (I heard the litter-bearers chattering before we climbed on board — the lady, the cat, and me) and I had heard that the Emperor himself lived there, so I was apprehensive. When the Lady Poppaea saw, she patted me on the head. "I won't let the Big, Bad Emperor see you," she said. "Anyhow, where we are going, the Emperor would *never* set foot in a million years. We are about to visit one of the people he hates the most."

I could imagine Himself hating many people. I did not wish to speculate, and the journey to the Oppian was up and down and winding, so I tried to make myself small. We found ourselves at the side entrance of what appeared to be a sprawling estate. It was, indeed, the Imperial Palace … not the Golden House you know today, but still vast. I realized that the likelihood of bumping into Himself the Divinity was small indeed.

The Lady Poppaea's litter was waved through more than one gateway, the sentries all appearing to recognize it. Or perhaps they recognized Hercules, peering through the curtain with slightly bared teeth.

At length we reached a kind of anteroom and the Lady Poppaea, the cheetah, and I stepped out of the litter. She motioned me to hover in the background. It was all I could to hold on to Hercules, as there were a few peacocks strutting about. In the room, slaves were scurrying about, throwing dresses into chests, packing up jewels and statuettes, all in great haste. Directing them was a stately woman with extremely tall hair, simply but expensively attired in silk.

She barely glanced at Poppaea, and not at all at the cheetah, let alone me. She merely moved quietly about the room, quietly commanding her slaves, who obeyed her swiftly and noiselessly.

Presently a slave brought the Lady Poppaea a jar of water. No wine. The other lady did not address us. It was a kind of game between her and Poppaea. Whoever acknowledged the other first would lose. I could see, however, that there was a great deal waiting to be said between them. The Lady Poppaea had brought me for a reason, not just to lead her pet on a leash. It seemed that she was too high and mighty to speak first. So, I approached the woman. The cheetah caused a bit of sensation and her slaves stifled screams as they tried to go about their business.

"Domina," I said.

"Impertinence!" said Lady Poppaea, slapping my face. At the exact same moment, the grand lady said, "Let him speak!"

I rubbed my cheek. If it was just for show, I wondered why she had to hit me quite so hard.

"I never realized you had a twin, Poppaea," said the Lady. "You should have dressed up that way. So … child … are you a true twin, or do you have a penis?"

"He has, for the time being, Octavia. How much longer, I do not know."

Octavia! This statuesque, very proper woman was no less than the Empress of Rome, the Lady Claudia Octavia.

I fell to the ground, almost losing my grip on Hercules's leash.

"Such nonsense. Get up, you snivelling brat. Your mistress has come to gloat. I know it. She won't have the pleasure. I will not speak to her."

"You needn't prostrate yourself to the Lady Claudia Octavia, you silly boy. She's in disgrace. Being sent off to exile on some remote island. Not sure which island, but it's *very* remote … and *small.* Smaller than this room, I would imagine."

"Let's take a look at you, you little freak of nature," Lady Octavia said, pulling me to my feet … the cheetah snarled. "Oh, Hercules, darling," said the Lady, who obviously knew the creature. "Let go the little boy." She called one of her women. "Lavinia, get one of the guards to come in and hold the leash for a while. One of those big hairy Germans. Or a pretty tall black one. One of each, better."

Two guards came in and took the cheetah off my hands. They stood at some distance, between two Corinthian columns.

"Tell the former Empress that I do not gloat … no more than one would expect. I'm not unnecessarily cruel. It's a fact that you have to be sent away, but it is no more than required by my ambitions. No, I'm not cruel. Selfish, yes. Not cruel."

The Lady Claudia Octavia did not look at the Lady Poppaea Sabina. Instead, she stared straight into my eyes. "Tell your mistress," she said, "that she is entering the demon's lair. No cheetahs ... he is a creature far more monstrous. His enemies don't even dare say his name ... rather, they take the numerological *gematria* to reduce NERON KAISAR to the number Six Hundred and Sixty-Six. People think that he imagines himself a God, even before the senate has deified him ... but he *is* a God. To enter his presence is to be consumed alive. He is the God of Death. Only another God can mate with him and live."

"Tell the ex-Divinitas," Poppaea said to me, "that bloated fantasies about mythical beings can't hide the simple fact that she is simply too *boring* to be Empress."

"Kindly inform Her Incoming Imperial Majesty," said the Lady Octavia, "that I may be boring, but I am the who carries the bloodline of the Julio-Claudian Dynasty. Divorcing me delegitimizes his birthright. He may be worshipped now, but he won't be after he's dead."

"And what *is* there after he is dead? What does it matter?" Poppaea said, accidentally addressing the Lady Octavia in person and thus, as it were, losing the competition. Suddenly aware of this, she stopped herself. "We should leave," she said to me. "Go and get Hercules."

"I haven't finished," Octavia said, seizing my shoulders. "You tell that ... *whore* that I am the one loved by the Roman rabble. The people look at me and see past doddering Claudius, past twisted Caligula, past that dull pervert Tiberius, and they see in my eyes Germanicus, the beloved, Augustus, the moral, and Julius Caesar, who left three hundred sesterces to every plebeian in his will. Divorcing me also divorces him from the right to be Emperor. The mob loves *me*. And without the mob, where is power? So, Nero is bundling me off in secret. Not to some island, as she insists, but to Campania. Doubtless she'll whisper in his ear and I'll end up on an island. Or I'll be killed. But the people's love for me won't be killed as easily. Nor their hatred for *you*," she added, finally turning to stab her finger in Poppaea's face.

The two of them stood like that, two frozen Furies, personifications of sheer rage.

Then, suddenly, they both started laughing.

"Enough drama," said the Lady Octavia. "Have a drink. I'm not long for this world … and neither are you, Poppaea. I don't really envy you."

"Well it will have been glorious while it lasted. And maybe I'll be tough to kill. Like Nero's mother. How many tries did it take? Tsk-tsk!"

"He rigged her ship to collapse and drown her, and she managed to swim ashore," Octavia said, laughing.

"And installing a machine in her ceiling to drop tiles on her while she slept!"

"And poisoning her *three* times, only she guessed in advance and swallowed an antidote first…."

"Finally, faking her suicide."

I wondered why an Emperor needed to go to such lengths to kill someone, even his own mother. Later I would learn far more than I ever needed to know, about the labyrinthine love-hate between mother and son, and from his own lips.

"All right," Octavia said at last. "It's a sad thing we're not still children. Do you remember …"

"Stealing the old tutors' tunicae from the bathhouse? Seeing them run howling down the street?" Poppaea giggled.

"Pouring the pepper in Nero's dormice! Ah! That slave got whipped to death for our prank," Octavia said, cackling. "I've had a good run. And now, I'm off to obscurity, stale bread, and the loom."

"It's a pity."

"I forgive you," said the Lady Octavia. "That's what you want, isn't it?"

On the journey back to our side of the hill, I asked the Lady Poppaea if the Lady Octavia was her friend.

She said, "Childhood is a magic time."

I said, "You won't need me any more. Whatever it is you were planning to get the Emperor, it worked."

"That's true, Sporus," she said. "While we were whiling away the morning at the Oppian Hill, Otho will already have packed. He is being made governor of Lusitania."

"Where's that?"

"Somewhere, you know, with wild tribes, warriors rubbing themselves with bear fat. The Celts are quite into buggery; Diodorus wrote that their warriors lie on the skins of animals, with 'a catamite on either side.' He'll be in heaven, the poor dear."

"So will his wife," I said softly.

"I shall be a goddess. There it is. It's a pity about Octavia, but goddesses need sacrifices."

It would be some time before I laid eyes on the Lady Claudia Octavia once more. And it would be in the form of a decapitated head, delivered to the Empress Poppaea in a golden casket.

XVII
HYACINTH

When I arrived, I was certain I would finally get that whipping I had avoided all these months. I had been all over the city, from Poppaea's villa to the apartments of the Empress herself, and after witnessing that altercation, all was not over, for Poppaea was not about to drop me off on her way back; Romans do not cater to the convenience of slaves, even those they are fond of.

At the home of Marcus Salvius Otho, it seemed that Poppaea's soon-to-be ex-husband had not yet departed. He was packing up everything that was not nailed down. Greek vases, statues, even the household lares and penates were being bundled into carts.

"You can't take those," Lady Poppaea was shrieking as she stepped from the litter. "Who will protect us?" She started slapping one of the slaves who was carrying a bulky statue. The confused boy dropped the statue and it cracked. Poppaea screamed and a steward hustled the unfortunate lad off for a whipping. His screams punctuated the ensuing conversation.

They would not move the carts out of the city until nightfall, now, thanks to the legal provision against wheeled traffic during daylight.

Otho looked at me, his eyes beady with concupiscence. "One final sojourn in my wife's pretty little forest," he said.

"He's not your wife, you bastard," Poppaea said.

But Otho ripped my tunic and violated me right in the vestibule. I was screaming, the whipped boy was screaming from another room, and Poppaea was screaming, while Otho mercilessly had at me. He climaxed very quickly, then flung me to the floor like old laundry. I lay there whimpering while husband and wife quarrelled.

"I don't see why you're complaining," Poppaea was saying. "Lusitania's an excellent posting."

"It's practically Britannia," Otho said, "and I don't like garum."

"You'll learn to. By the time you get home, you'll have fish sauce running in your veins," Poppaea sniggered.

"Bitch!"

"Look who's talking," Poppaea. "You practically ripped that boy a new arsehole. And his old one won't be any use for days."

It is easy to forget that, however generous and compassionate and loving they are when they've a mind to it, they still don't think of you as a human being. I was sobbing on the cold stone floor, and no one cared.

"Remember, Poppaea darling, that the higher you rise, the more hideous your fall will be. And if the likes of you can become an Empress, then *I* could be an Emperor one day — and when I do, I'll have you in the arena, being raped to death by wolves."

"Oh, you do so terrify me, you spineless little *cinaedus*."

"You dare call me that! You know I always take the active role in intercourse."

"You've never taken *any* role, to my knowledge,"

Poppaea said. "At least not with me."

He slapped her face.

"Bold, aren't you? You forget I'm the Empress."

"Not quite."

"And I won't forget how you brazenly speculated about becoming Emperor yourself! That, my darling, is treason. You could be thrown off the Tarpeian Rock for that, and you know I have the Emperor's ear."

"You do not! You only have his cock!"

"That is all one needs," said the Lady Poppaea Sabina, smiling sweetly. And finally saw me, weeping on the marble. "Don't be tiresome, Sporus," she said to me, pulling me to my feet.

"I'm in pain, domina."

"There, there." She clapped her hands and her steward appeared from behind a curtain. "Send the boy home, will you? And give him a tip. A *big* tip. I've really worn him out today, not to mention he'll probably catch a dose of the strap when he Petronius finds out he's almost a day late."

The steward bowed and led me out. I could still hear the soon-to-be-divorced couple shrieking at each other when I reached the front door. I was soon alone in the Lady Poppaea's private litter with the curtains drawn, with a heavy pouch of silver denarii to count.

The words of Marcus Salvius Otho were prophetic, were they not? For he did *become Emperor. For a day or two at least.*

Yes, and even such as I became Empress, too, *twice!* — so you could say I was twice the goddess Poppaea ever was. And my violent death will be witnessed by more than twice as many people as Poppaea's ignominious end.

What a distinction!

Quiet.

Hear that menacing sound, like a cat's purr, only deeper, hungrier? They're delivering some fresh lions.

Haven't they run out of Christians yet?

Fresh batch.

Let's go and visit. Come on. I'm not exactly going to run away, not with my feet shackled like this.

I had resigned myself to more pain when I finally crossed the limen of my master's house. Though it was still daylight, there was a pall. Slaves looked at me and looked away. I saw Croesus go by and he did not even see me. I saw my master in the atrium and went to prostrate myself.

"Domine," I knelt at his feet, trying to frame an excuse for why I was so late getting home. "Domine, the Lady Poppaea made me go with her to gloat at the Empress on her way to exile."

Petronius did not seem at all interested. "Go to the slaves' quarters," he told me. "They'll tell you all about it. Leave me alone."

I slunk away and went down to the basement. Outside my cell, there were many members of the household gathered. I pushed through to the open door and saw Hyacinth on his pallet. His lower body was drenched in blood. A thin sheet covered his loins but it was dripping. Hyacinth was shaking and losing blood and I knew he was going to die.

I immediately realized what had happened.

Croesus came now, and the others fell back a little. I turned on him. "You let him have it done!" I was angry and I didn't care if he knew. "You didn't care about risking his life!"

"Sporus," Hyacinth said, so softly I had to strain to hear, "I used my peculium."

The other slaves were murmuring about how no one knew, how Hyacinth had sneaked away in the middle of the night and gone to some street surgeon who worked on slaves and criminals. I lay down next to Hyacinth and tried to warm him. Warm, sticky blood seeped into my tunica.

"By the time we knew," Croesus said, "he had already lost so much blood...."

"What about a doctor?" I said.

"I sent Hylas to fetch one."

"Some butcher from the market?"

Croesus said, "No, no. The best the household budget will stretch to. I haven't dared to ask the dominus for more because the boy did this on his own initiative. Meaning he damaged the master's property."

"What, he'll punish him for injuring himself?"

"No ... no ... he'll punish *us* for breaking something so precious."

Again, for me alone to hear, Hyacinth said, "Send me to our gods, Sporus. I don't want to rot in a Roman cave. I want to go whole to my Skyfather." He used a name for the chieftain of the gods that I had not heard since the village. When I heard that name, the tears started to come, and I couldn't stop them.

I ran from the room to seek out Petronius. I found him burning incense by the herm in the atrium garden. "Domine, domine," I said, "can't we do something?"

"Did Croesus not summon a doctor?"

"He has, but not a *proper* one." I knelt at his feet once

more, just as I had when I begged him not to send me away. I clasped his waist, I buried my face in his groin. "We have to save him," I said.

"Come," he said. "This time your pretty head against my manhood is not going to work. This is Ananke ... it is fate, my Giton."

He raised me to my feet and kissed me gently on the forehead.

"I did not want to see him at first. I keep no broken vases in my house, no shattered statues ... some do, because they are old things found in Greece and redolent with ancient magic ... I don't like to look at things that cannot be fixed. But your tears move me, Sporus."

The dominus and I went down to the slaves' quarters. It was clear that Petronius did not know his way down there in the basement, even though it was his own house. The odor disturbed him, too, though he did not mention it. I led him by the hand to my cell; he had not bothered to know where I slept, when I was not sleeping in his room.

When Petronius entered, the slaves, unbidden, knelt; even Hyacinth struggled to perform an obeisance, but the effort was too much for him and he slumped back. I rushed to his side. But he was already breathing his last.

"He loved you, domine," I said, not hiding my anger. "He did this to himself so you wouldn't throw him away." I glared at my master, heedless of any chastisement, while the other slaves shrank back, appalled at my audacity.

Then I knelt next to the cement bed and kissed Hyacinth on the lips, with that act drawing away his soul and setting him free.

Gaius Petronius Arbiter did not order me whipped. In fact, he said nothing at all, at first. And then, softly, so I was the only one who heard, "What right did he have to love me? No freeborn ever loved me enough to die for me."

And he turned abruptly and began to walk away.

At that moment, Hylas arrived with the doctor. He looked at me, and he looked at Hyacinth, and he knew. The doctor, seeing the dominus, bowed deeply and scurried away.

"I'll send for the libitinarius," Croesus said, but the dominus wasn't even listening.

"What's that?" I whispered.

"The undertaker. It costs sixty sesterces to dispose of a dead slave."

"But he told me wants a real funeral. He wants to go back to the Skyfather. With no pieces missing."

"Sporus, don't offend the master. In his way he is grieving. But you know how he is. He won't look at a broken vase."

I didn't care. I caught up with the dominus by the stairs. "Ah, Sporus," he said. "Don't you dare do anything like that."

"I wouldn't dream of it, domine."

"This unpleasantness … it fouls the air. I will have to bring in a priest for a purification ceremony. The house will reek of incense and oils. I think I shall pack up early for the summer. Cheer up, my Giton. You will love Antium. The breezes, the gentle sun … you can swim in the sea. Your lovely skin will turn to bronze. Come to bed, Sporus. I don't want to wrestle with any of my women tonight. I want to hold you like a doll."

I knelt again, not caring if I offended. "Domine! Hyacinth asked me to ensure him a proper burial."

"Very well, then," Petronius said abstractedly. "We'll have the libitinarius stash him in the family columbarium. I never go there. It's somewhat distant from the city walls but I'll tip him extra."

"Master, he asked me to send him to *his* gods." Frustrated, I pulled out the huge pouch of silver that the Lady Poppaea's steward had given me. "Please, domine. The lady paid me well, because she took me with her to gloat over Claudia Octavia, and then her husband was very rough with me on his way out the door. I can pay for the funeral."

Petronius looked at the pouch. Took it, hefted it, then loosened the string. He saw it was mostly silver, with even the glint of an aureus or two … not one orichalcum in the whole bag.

"You would do this for him?"

And I heard the unspoken question: *But what would you do for me?*

"Don't you realize what a big piece of your freedom this is?" he said.

"I'm not an accountant. I'm just your puer delicatus."

"All right then," he said. "See to it."

He kept the money.

It was an important lesson. Hyacinth and I were like statues and vases. We were not people. Petronius loved me, indulged me … but he still owned me. And on some level, because he owned every inch of me, because he had the right to do anything he wanted to any part of me … he also feared me. Because the love of a thing you own is not the love a human being feels. It is a love whose roots are in fear. And fear always begets fear.

It was in that moment that I swore to myself: *I will be free.*

XVIII

ANTIUM

To speak of Antium is to speak of heaven, I suppose. Antium, Elysium on Earth, playground of the wealthy.

And from Petronius's villa it was only a few steps to the sea. The villa stood a little way off from the gargantuan Villa Neronis, separated by a wall of rock, and with its own little cove. The harbor itself, hidden from our view by a bend in the shoreline, was close enough to walk to. The air was clear ... there were none of the foul smells that rise from the Aventine in summer and suffocate the city and spread pestilence.

Petronius loved to be surrounded by beautiful things and this was such a place. But I was mourning Hyacinth, so I didn't run along the sand or jump into the waves. The others did. I sat on a rock. The strangeness of Hyacinth's funeral still haunted me.

Why, what are funerals like in your country? Are they very exotic? Slave girls sacrificed on a burning boat? A well-loved puppy buried alive in the dead one's arms? Brains removed through the nostrils and stored in a jar?

Exotic? Not to me.

You never even told me the name of your country.

It is far from Rome. And I don't want to think of it. Thinking about it when we said goodbye to Hyacinth was painful ... though it was three emperors ago ... it hurts more than anything else.

I am from Bithynia.

Never heard of it.

My dominus had said, "It's to your credit that you would delay your own freedom to give your friend the rites he would have wished for. I could simply pay it myself, as a favor to a much loved slave, but then I would not be granting your desire the dignitas it deserves. But I have only two conditions. First, no matter what your native customs are, I don't want you chopping off your hair or wandering around glumly. If you have to do the Greek thing with the rending of garments and the shrieking and wailing, keep it discreet and put on some makeup if I have guests. Also, we don't keep dead bodies in the house overnight, so anything you do, have Croesus first arrange for the libitinarius to take away and store the body elsewhere."

In the village where I lived, dead people stayed in the home for many days; we talked to them, made much of them, sat beside them and told them stories ... making sure that old wrongs were righted ... before an old man who spoke for our Skyfather came to take us to some hilltop, open to the embrace of heaven. After the burning, we scatter the ashes from the highest point in the vicinity.

But I did not say goodbye properly, because the Romans were anxious to purify the house. And Rome is a hilly place, but there are no hilltops open to the sky, for the best hilltops have palaces and mansions on them. It was difficult to find anyone of our people who knew the ways, or could speak the words as our village shaman might have done.

One person who helped me was Marcus Vinicius. He even found the woman called Spider for me; she was working at a lupanar, not as a prostitute, of course, for she was long past the age of marketing her womanhood; she was the one who collected the guests' money and exchanged it for spintriae, little bronze tokens with depictions of various sex acts on the obverse. Useful to show the whores what was to be expected, since often they did not even speak Latin.

"It's dull enough work," she said, "and the girls are a sorry lot. The boys aren't much better. Your friend must have imagined that life, and felt it was worth the risk to do what he did."

Hyacinth lay in the cart, packed in snow and ice — the ice was what had used up almost all of Lady Poppaea's tip, as by the time it gets to Rome you've already lost half of it, and snow is a delicacy when honeyed spiced syrups are dribbled over it — But with the heat ... I knew Hyacinth would want to look beautiful until the last minute.

"We had best be going," Marcus said, as he had paid for only that evening of Spider's time. We were gathered in front of Petronius's front door, waiting for sunset so that we could leave the city by cart. Of the household, only Hylas came. Spider had found the right shaman ... he had been working as a doorman at one of the houses where they keep their doormen chained to the front post ... he had a fugitive brand on his forehead. He spoke no Latin or

Greek, and had been much mistreated, as so often happens to those assumed to be idiots. But speaking to me in our own language, he was full of tales and he had spoken to the gods on many occasions; his words made me weep, even more than the spectacle of my dead friend packed in snow and ice in the glow of a Roman sunset.

Our sad processional moved slowly. The military escort was something Hyacinth would never have dreamed of when he was alive, but it was something Marcus's rank could command. Two hired link-boys with torches walked ahead. We passed the Circus Maximus, huge and gloomy. We moved through the slums in the Aventine and stopped at the Ostia Gate; we continued on foot to the designated high mountain....

But Mount Testaceus was not even a real hill, though it loomed up ahead as we walked in the moonlight. It had become a hill because this was where people had thrown their used amphorae for the last seven hundred years. It had plenty of vegetation, of course; trees' roots had worked their way through centuries of smashed wine-jugs. In the air hung the stale smell of old wine, laced with a whiff of human vomit. Our caligae crunched on the piles of potsherds.

I would be laying my friend to rest in a rubbish dump.

It was a bitter thing, more bitter because those who were in the position of being *domini* were trying so hard to give us room for our feelings. Each act of generosity came with an unconscious undertone of condescension, yet I had to take whatever I was given.

So there I was, in the glowing sunlight of Actium, my mind permeated with dark memories. I watched Hylas leaping up and down and wading near the shore. Petronius's women, too, were there, naked and of every hue, splashing each other and laughing.

In the distance I could see my master walking with the steward Croesus, deep in conversation. He stopped to look at the women, and at Hylas, and then at me. He summoned me with a crook of a finger and I went to him.

"Let me look at you," he said in a quizzical way.

"Domine," I said, "you speak as if you will never see me again."

"Oh," he said. "I will see you. But perhaps not in quite the same light as before."

It was a kind of inkling, then, of what the dominus was fond of quoting to me from the poet Virgil: *Tempus inreparabile fugit.* "What are you saying to me, domine?" I asked him. "Why not in the same light? Did I offend you in the matter of Hyacinth?"

"No, no, my Giton."

He put his arm around me and gently squeezed my bare back, which was already getting a little red from the sunlight. My skin's imperfection seemed to irk my dominus a little. But he drew me close and kissed me, very gently, on the lips, and again on the forehead, like a favorite child or puppy. My master always smelled of honey, with a subtle hint of frankincense. It was always comforting to fall asleep beside him.

"You should run along inside and have them put a poultice on that," he said. "I need you to look perfect tomorrow."

"Why, domine? Where are we going?"

"Look behind you. Looming over us on the hill."

I did. The sprawling Villa Neronis, the seaside residence

of the Emperor, sat astride the precipice. "We are going to dinner tomorrow."

"Surely ... not me, master! You've told me I have to make myself scarce, and not let the Emperor see me."

"I'm afraid it's an imperial order. The Lady Poppaea Sabina has specifically requested you. No longer the Lady Poppaea Sabina, but the Augusta."

"A slave at a royal banquet, and not there to serve?"

"We are all slaves," Petronius said, "when it comes to Divinitas. But you shall help me; you will carry my scroll, and look pretty so people do not weary of just my voice droning on and on. For I am to give a private reading of the Trimalchio scene from the book I have been writing, the *Satyricon*. This scene describes the most overblown banquet in all of history ... yet my wildest imaginings will be as nothing compared to the feast we are going to be attending. Many would willingly die to see what we will see. So, this 'little something' at the Villa Neronis. It's an invitation that cannot be refused. It's a 'small affair with just a few friends.' That's what Himself has decided to call it. It's a wedding banquet."

"No, master, not that!"

"No, my delicatus, don't clasp my knees and beg again. I can't let you hide in a cat-box this time. I may not be able to do anything at all to prevent what will happen ... without risking ... *everything*."

"You mustn't risk anything, master," I said. No, I thought, not for a favorite vase. Or would he smash it rather than give it away? For he *was* going to give me away. That *had* to be it.

Troubled, perhaps, my master turned to Croesus. "About the papers I asked to be drawn up, Croesus," he began ...

and I could tell that I was being dismissed.

My mind was a blur as I walked back to my rock. After all, whose wedding could the Emperor be celebrating but his own wedding to the Lady Poppaea? Poppaea who had engineered the banishment of the Lady Claudia Octavia — a scion of the true blood of Augustus — and the dismissal of Lord Otho to rule some faraway province? And had Poppaea not demanded *me* as a wedding gift? Was this why my master was looking at me with such regret? Was I the favorite vase that must be given away? Or would he rather smash me to pieces than let someone else have me?

Would I now be another decoration in Lady Poppaea's home ... the home of an Empress? A woman with infinite power over the whole world, let alone my insignificant self?

"You. Come in this water," I heard Hylas call. "Warm. Good."

But I demurred, plunging instead into the ocean of memory ... thinking of Hyacinth, lying on the crude bier, surrounded by broken wine pots. I brushed away the last pieces of ice. There was no breeze to scatter the stench of vinegar and old puke.

Into his hands, I placed the small pouch that contained what he had had cut off. He had to be whole to go to the embrace of Skyfather. Hylas bent down to put a loaf of bread and some olives beside the body. "You eat good in sky," he said softly.

I placed next to his face the mirror fragment that Spider had once given me.

She looked oddly at me, as if to say, How could you give away my gift to you?

I said to her, "This piece of mirror showed me myself for the first time. But now, I don't think I need to see myself anymore. But Hyacinth ... he wanted to stay young and beautiful a little longer. Now it'll be forever. But me, I don't have a self that I yearn to see. I'm whatever other people see, nothing more. I am their mirror. I don't need to *have* a mirror anymore."

I stayed silent for the rest of the funeral. Hylas spoke a few words in broken Latin. The wise old man spoke a great deal, but his words were arcane, and though it was my mother tongue, the language seemed more and more alien to me. Even Spider spoke, warmly, like a mother.

When Hyacinth was consumed in the flames, I climbed the mountain of smashed pots to its highest point, to scatter the ashes at the sky, to make it easy for the gods to reach down and scoop him to their bosom.

But I still said nothing. It was not grief that prevented me from speaking, nor was it regret at the shortness of the time I had spent with him. It was anger. And envy. Hyacinth had gone somewhere where perhaps he could be happy. And he had left me behind.

And now, sitting in the golden sunset at the shore of Antium, even more unsure of my future than I was when a pirate captured and sold me ... now I felt the anger even more keenly. And the utter helplessness.

XIX

Praefectus

"A little event, for a few close friends?"

I cannot wait for you to tell me of the party! What a spectacle it must have been! The extravagance! The decadence!

Did you ever read my master's book, *Satyricon?* It does not begin to describe what we saw. There must have been a thousand people at this little gathering, though, to be sure, a lot of them were there to serve: the cupbearers, each one more beautiful than Ganymede, the pageboy of the King of Heaven; the dancing girls, somersaulting over silver chargers piled with exotic roasted animals, the water-organ, the duelling orchestras from opposite sides of the hall ... the jugglers, the fire-eaters, and matched pairs of armed men fighting to the death, mostly ignored by the guests ... and in the center of it all, on a dais raised above the rest ... *Himself, the Divinitas, the Master of the World.* A

Greek *kithara* in his arms, strumming now and then, while beautiful women and boys fed him the most delicate of morsels.

He wasn't this bloated lump you see on the last coins of the reign, you know. He was pretty; almost beautiful. No, beautiful is not too strong a word. The presentation ensured that. His radiance illuminated all the world, in the flickering of a thousand torches. The jowls, the scowl, they all came later.

It was then, perhaps, that the Emperor first laid eyes on you properly ... and you so seduced him with your siren wiles that eventually you became Empress?

Hardly that. If anyone was seduced, it was me. Not my Emperor, my God. For it takes a lot of hard work ... and a great deal of bad luck ... to win the love of a living God.

Reaching the Villa Neronis was easy, if strenuous; Petronius's own villa was tucked away in a cove, invisible from the royal enclave but actually easily accessible by steps cut into the cliff. It was too steep for a litter, but close enough on foot. Gaius Petronius brought a very small entourage; two slaves to hold the scroll of *Satyricon,* which was kept in a glazed amphora slung over their shoulders; me, to look pretty and adoring when the dominus read, and for some reason I could not yet fathom, Croesus.

When we entered the Villa Neronis, we had to pass through several colonnades, and to be looked over by impressive guards at each post. The uniforms became grander at each station. Finally we approached a throne room through a portico lined with the greatest art treasures stolen from the greatest fallen empires of the past, from Babylon to Egypt, and what seemed to be the complete statuary of a couple of plundered Greek temples.

And this was only the Emperor's *country* house.

Not the *Golden House* that was to come.

There were, as it were, several circles of guests, orbiting the Emperor, presumably the farther away being the less favored. The couch we were directed to was directly in front of Himself, in the inner circle. On the uppermost level were the Divinitas, the Lady Poppaea Sabina, with Hercules crouching at her feet, a sturdy-looking Nubian in the background holding onto his leash; there was Tigellinus, in whose house I had once been, and Pythagoras, who had once serviced the royal posterior in public, but was now relegated to standing behind the Divinitas with a tray of olives. I also saw Lucan, and was surprised he seemed to be enjoying higher favor than my master; though of course, he was younger and prettier.

We were to dine directly beneath the gaze of Himself the Divinity, meaning I would be seen at all times. And I was not naked, the normal garb of the puer delicatus. Petronius had made me wear a blindingly white tunic with a fresh, heady scent of urine, having just come from the laundry. Counteracting the fragrance of piss was the fact that my hair had been slathered with a pomatum composed of bear fat, laced with attar of roses.

When we arrived, a bevy of dark beauties from some far unconquered country were leaping and dancing to drums and choral singing in an exotic language full of clicks. Right in front of the Emperor, two hefty amazons were wrestling in a trough of mud. In the distance, an orchestra of bucinae and tubae squalled and screeched to the pounding of a tympanum.

As we took our seats, one woman warrior was having

her neck broken, and the entire trough, with the other standing triumphant and sweaty, was carried off; the violent entertainment was replaced by a bard with a lyre. The bard sang a song by the immortal Sappho, one I had before in the house of Petronius:

As a mountain wind
Sweeps down upon an oak-tree
Love shook my heart

The haunting, antique melismata echoed in the hall and at once the shrieking brass and thudding percussion from the other end seemed to fade so that it sounded like a throbbing heartbeat. Still magical after six hundred years, the Aeolic cadences of the Lesbian poetess hung in the air, and gossip was silenced.

After the poetry, the actual nuptials were almost perfunctory. A priest came in, the Empress and Emperor recited the ritual formula:

Ubi tu Gaius, ibi ego Gaia …
Where thou art Gaius, I am Gaia.

There was general applause and cheering, but the feast could not have been interrupted for more than a few moments, for as soon as the applause ended, the bucinae blared and pies the size of chariot wheels were brought in; a chef at each table slashed them open and songbirds burst out of every one of them, filling the air with trilling melodies and, it must also be said, raining down droppings upon our heads. This was received with more applause … even the hapless guests who happened to have been shit upon took it all in good fun, though their laughter may have been laced with fear of the Emperor's displeasure.

"This wedding's nothing," a voice piped up from the next table down, on the next circle beyond ours. "When I was posted to Judaea, now *those* people had weddings that lasted for days! People think of the Jews as crude barbarians, but they certainly knew how to have a good time, when they weren't revolting!"

Petronius and I looked over. It was an old man in a somewhat frayed toga. The entire table, in fact, was occupied by such old men, some in military uniform. My dominus said to me, "That man used to be the praefectus of Judaea, a very long time ago. I thought he was dead. I see that entire table is populated with several generations of generals. Look ... Galba ... Vitellius ... Vespasianus ... they're probably plotting a coup."

He waved at the man who had been speaking. "Didn't know you were still alive, Pilatus," he said.

"I've been living in retirement for thirty years," he said. "But I might make a comeback."

Petronius laughed, and whispered to me, "He was recalled in disgrace, but with a change of Emperors, disgrace became oblivion."

Pilatus turned away from us and continued to regale his companions. "They're constantly revolting," he said, "as Vespasianus here knows. And they have a folk belief that a king will arise and drive us away from the land, which, apparently, their God gave them. I had to crucify at least one of these messiahs every week! There was one my wife rather liked, although he gave her nightmares...."

I became aware that the Lady Poppaea was standing between our table and the praefectus's as he started to speak of a cannibalistic, blood-drinking sect he called *Chrestianoi.* "Totally godless," he was saying. "Won't even worship the Emperor! Can you imagine!"

At length the Lady Poppaea seemed to find the old men's war stories tiresome, and turned to us.

Or, rather, to me. She looked at me, very pointedly, and Hercules was pulling at the Nubian's leash; the cheetah wanted me to pet him.

"I'm glad you came," she said to me. "Even though your favorite fat rapist is all the way in Lusitania."

"I could hardly not bring him," Petronius said. "An imperial invitation is a divine command."

To my alarm, I saw that Another was looking at me, too. Himself the Divinity, from his lofty vantage point, was scrutinizing me through a giant emerald held up to a squinting eye.

"Indeed," said the Lady Poppaea. "Oh! Petronius, too," she added, almost as an afterthought.

"My lady," he said.

"I see you've brought your wedding gift," she said to Petronius, "just as I requested."

I looked at my master in alarm. Was I going to be handed over right now, in front of a thousand people, gift-wrapped in my piss-pungent brand new tunic?

The Lady took my hand and pulled me up from the couch. "Shall I take him up to the Emperor now? I trust you've brought the deed of gift?" I looked past her to the Emperor. I could not help myself. He was truly the center of the universe.

Petronius waved Croesus over. He had a little scroll in

his hand. Poppaea cackled. My heart sank.

"Divinity," said my master, bowing almost to the floor, "I do have a gift for Himself, one worthy of greatness. But I won't in fact be presenting him with this boy."

"You are reneging on your promise?"

"I did say I would give you my slave, Lady Poppaea. But Sporus is not my slave," he said, unrolling the scroll. "As you will see from this little document, the articles of manumission went into effect yesterday. Sporus is free."

I broke into tears. I fell prostrate and kissed my master's feet.

XX

LIBERTAS

I was shaken. And shaking, too, because when I got up off the floor, I was a different person … a different *species*, indeed, for I was no longer an object, but a human being. Yet I felt no different. At least, not in that moment.

An omelette with peacocks' brains and honey was being carried in, accompanied by another fanfare on brass and tympanum.

Poppaea Sabina had not ceased to look, rather, glare at me, and I could see she was already seeing this defeat as a temporary annoyance. She did not fly into a rage. What she said, however, was bone-chilling. "I am not my husband. He's a passionate creature, quick to have a tantrum and to cry afterwards about his friend he accidentally had beheaded in a fit of pique. I'm more of a … cold, slow, heartless, vengeance-minded kind of woman. So I will say only this to you, Petronius Arbiter: you know very well how this will end. Not immediately, because we are civilized people, by the Gods; we've managed to crawl our way into the Ninth Century since Romulus and Remus. We are Romans, cheerfully falling on our swords or slitting our wrists at the merest whisper of a stain to our honour. So, what are you really telling us, Petronius Arbiter? And is it worth it?"

"There is no guile. Sporus is a much-loved member of my household. I'm even letting him keep his peculium. I'll set him up in one of the hideous slum apartments I own in the suburra, or he'll just remain in my service and living in my household."

"And what will he do? What he did for me and Otho? Diminishing returns, you know. The older he gets, the cheaper."

"You're wrong, Divinity. And I only dare to contradict you because we've known each other so long. Sporus is coming along very nicely in languages, and if he ever loses his looks he could do well managing a library, interpreting for diplomats, negotiating with foreign merchants, and what have you. He's already as bright as Croesus."

"And as rich?" said the Lady Poppaea, making the usual joke about Croesus's name.

"One day, perhaps," my master said. "But it is his choice. He may go into the service of the Divinity if he wishes. He may choose. That is what freedom means."

"You silly man," said Poppaea. "We are all slaves … even the Emperor."

"Indeed," said Petronius Arbiter, "you are perceptive, Divinity."

"Let's listen to some more of what old Pilatus has to say," said the Lady Poppaea, and she leaned against the back of our couch, just within earshot of where the generals were telling their war stories.

"Is it true, Pilatus," she said, "that the Chrestianoi kill and eat babies?"

"Oh, far more appalling than that!" he said, laughing. "They practise licentious *orgia,* which they call love-feasts, in the catacombs, in the dark, amongst the decaying corpses. But they do worse than eating babies … they actually eat the flesh of their god."

"A delicacy, I should think, if you could ever get it."

"But everyone hates them, and of all the silly oriental cults in Rome, theirs is one of the dullest, though they do give me some recognition for having crucified their leader, some madman."

It seemed that the other military men found him tedious, and had their own stories to tell, more recent and more bloody, for they soon started talking over him.

"I have something even more scandalous," said General Vitellius, "another subversive poem by Antistius Sosianus that has been discovered, comparing the Divinitas unfavorably to the faeces of a goose. The Emperor should never have spared his life…."

You saw Vitellius! You laid eyes on him who is now Himself the Divinity, the fourth Emperor we have had in a single year!

How was I to know? He was just some general. I barely glanced at this Vitellius, and perhaps I should have, since it was he who eventually condemned me to die in this ignominious theatrical display….

Ah, he was the Emperor who was to be your undoing.

Indeed. Well, he was fat.

It was Petronius's turn to perform, and I followed him to the Emperor's dais. My master opened up the scroll of his book and began to read. In this passage from his unfinished manuscript, Petronius spoke of a freedman named Gaius Pompeius Trimalchio Maecenatianus, who was throwing the most extravagant, tasteless, vulgar banquet one could imagine.

Gaius Petronius's voice was quite singular; though his narrative voice was deep, he modulated his tones, now sounding like the handsome Encolpius, now the simpering wife, Fortunata, now the brash, self-aggrandising Trimalchio. You could taste the pigs' carcasses into which were sewn living birds that the guests had to run about catching … a dish for every sign in the zodiac … hares with feathers stuck in their backs to represent Pegasus … meat carvers who wielded their knives with the panache of a secutor with a gladius in the arena. It all came magically alive, just with words. Although the chamber was huge, conversation became hushed. A thousand people were hanging on my master's words. And there I was, holding the scroll open, displaying myself in my tunic of virginal whiteness to a God - to the only God who mattered in the real world.

The food and spectacle of Petronius's novel may not have been as epic as the Emperor's banquet, but his words unlocked more colors, textures and sounds than could be found in ten such banquets. The reading had the effect of making the feast we were at, in all its extravagance, seem drab and devoid of color. Petronius did not just use the elegant language of an Ovid or the metaphoric flights of Sappho. His palette also made liberal use of gutter talk, the slang of prostitutes, the gruffness of soldiers, the patois of unlettered slaves.

And in the Emperor's eyes I saw not just admiration, but also … resentment. And I also saw that my master did not care. He had deliberately stepped over a line, as surely as

Julius Caesar had when he crossed the Rubicon a hundred years ago, setting in motion events that would bring the Republic crashing down.

The Lady Poppaea Sabina had not been wrong. My master had the air of someone who has seen his own death.

Finally Petronius's reading came to an end and there was thunderous applause. The Divinitas, too, applauded languidly. The Empress clapped her hands a few times, and yawned.

"Brilliant, Petronius," said Nero. "You truly are a marvel. Of course, you quite overshadowed my own little meal."

"Perhaps so," said Petronius, walking a very careful tightrope. "But if our audience were to hear one of *your* compositions now, my own little recitation will pale into insignificance."

"I do have a little something planned," said the Emperor.

"I await with bated breath, Divinitas. But meanwhile...."

With a flourish, Petronius motioned for his slaves to bring the special amphora that was made to hold the scroll, and they laid it at the Emperor's feet.

"A tasteful presentation, as usual," said Himself the Divinity, "but Poppaea gave me to understand that the wedding gift was going to include the boy."

"The Divine Empress must not have realized, Divinitas, that I've actually given this delicatus his freedom. I regret that I'm unable to give that which I don't possess."

"Well, then I'll accept the freely given gift from the hands of the gift itself," said the Emperor, whom one did not, of course, contradict.

What was I to do? I had been free for only an hour. Would I now have to declare myself a slave again? Lady Poppaea had a look of triumph, and she launched into the Medusa-like cackle I'd heard her use on her ex-husband. "Choose, you silly child," she said, "and mind you make the right choice, because your master's fate lies in your answer!"

I was going to stand my ground. I was going to say that, no matter what, my loyalty was to my former dominus. I know that's what he wanted me to say. "I should really be your enemy, Petronius," said the Emperor, "but you're simply not important enough."

But at that moment, a steward came to whisper in the Empress's ear. Her cackling became shriller, even more raucous. "You've been upstaged, Petronius!" she said. "I have received an even better wedding gift than a twin sister with a penis."

More blaring bucinae now, and a dozen soldiers marched in lockstep into the room, escorting an enormous, covered platter wrought in gold.

"I'll deal with you later," said the Emperor to Petronius, and our party backed away, stepped down to our level, leaving the amphora with Petronius's precious creation unattended and forgotten.

To the beat of the tympanum, and the erotic wailings of double-flutes, the soldiers approached. As my master and his entourage, including me, returned to their places, the platter was set in front of the two Divinitates. It took two soldiers to lift the cover.

Squealing with delight, the Empress of Rome seized her gift and held it aloft … by the hair. There were scattered screams and titters … no applause, and for that I thanked the gods that there was still a shred of human decency in this depraved crowd. But the collective gasp of the crowd had a kind of vampiric hunger to it.

It had been packed with salt for the journey, but I still recognized the decapitated head of the Lady Claudia Octavia, who had once been Empress of Rome, the most direct in the tortuous line of the Julio-Claudian family ... descended through Julius Caesar from Aeneas himself, and through him from the goddess Venus.

I was sitting so close I could hear the flies.

Then spoke Nero Claudius Caesar Augustus Germanicus. "Time, I think," he said, "to clear the air. I shall perform an ode I have composed, quite apposite, I think, for it honors the ancestry of the late Empress ... *my* ancestry ... for I am the adopted son of Claudius, son of Germanicus, son of ... all the way back to the Prince Aeneas, son of Venus, who fled the burning fires of Troy. Let what I sing to you be a paean not only of death, but of rebirth. For Rome, like the phoenix, ever springs up from its own ashes, does it not?"

A hush fell over the room. It was as profound as the silence that accompanied by dominus's recitation. But where that silence came from fascination, from the seductive storytelling in my master's *Satyricon*, this was a silence birthed in stark terror.

"Before I begin," said Himself the Divinity, "I shall quote the immortal Virgil, who said, *'Infandum, regina, iubes renovare dolorem'* — *'O Queen, you bid me renew unspeakable grief.'* You, my adoring public, shall decide whether the Queen I address is the late Augusta, or the current one."

A long, pregnant pause.

He was about to touch a finger to the *kithara* when

another messenger arrived. Nero waited. He did not, apparently, want his opening chord to be ruined by some jarring message. The messenger was unbathed and had obviously been riding at top speed. He lurched through the guests and up to Himself without ceremony, and gave his message so quietly that perhaps not even Poppaea heard it.

Nero stood. "We are moving this banquet to Rome," he said. "Poppaea, see that all the guests accompany us. Tell the army to mobilize every chariot, every oxcart. We're leaving right away."

"Now, my Lord?" she said. "There's another thirty-seven courses. Whatever for?"

"I'm told there's a better venue for my world premiere," he said.

The whispers became a roar and I caught a word here and there, and this is how I learned that Rome was burning.

XXI

Per Ignem

It is forty-three *mille passuum* from Antium to Rome, thus four or five hours even at a trot. For a time, our procession was able to keep up this clip, for the Praetorians rode ahead, driving the riff-raff off the road. But as we approached the city, our caravan slowed to a crawl, even with an Emperor, for even armed soldiers cannot easily ram through a torrent of panicking plebeians.

We could feel the heat even before we could see the city. Three miles from Rome along the Via Appia, the journey became really tough going. Petronius and I and our small party were crammed into a horse-cart with several other poets, most of them drunk.

The Praetorians rode ahead at a steady trot, lashing people out of the way in the wake of Himself, resplendent on a golden chariot whose driver was dressed as Icarus … the cart I was in was not far behind. Riders, with torches held aloft, escorted our convoy.

But by now all the traffic was in the opposite direction, a sea of refugees, carrying all their possessions. Weeping, wailing, snivelling children, old men, pack animals …

none of the able-bodied men, for doubtless they were helping the vigiles to put out the fire. We moved as swiftly as we could.

Our party had suffered considerable attrition since leaving Antium. While few would think to openly contradict the Divinity's commands, it was clear that some hoped that in the pandemonium, Himself would not notice an absence or two. Yet the road was still packed with the guests who had not dared refuse, in their carts or on horseback, and with vehicle after vehicle piled high with luxury foods. Sweetmeats were packed tightly into snow. Other carts contained the stacked carcasses of creatures yet to be roasted. Cages with squawking peacocks waiting to be brained. Amphorae filled with live lampreys. Hares, turtles, monkeys, any exotic creature that could be eaten … all were part of our procession. From time to time, the band of bucinae blared away.

The heat we felt first, but now came the glow, too. The horizon was ablaze. The wind seared our faces. Our caravan circumvented the closest gate and went right, around the Servian Wall until it reached the Porta Esquilina, mounting the city, as it were, from the rear.

We snaked up the Esquiline. The sky glowed, but the wind and smoke were being borne away from us, that is until we reached the valley and had to start climbing once more, this time the Palatine.

And now, the full majesty and terror hove into view as we reached the summit. The building we reached was at the edge of the imperial complex. There were already people gathered, members of the household, and the Praetorians began barking commands. Couches were brought in. We were gathering on a huge veranda that overlooked the burning city.

It was madness, but slaves were scurrying like rats to have the banquet continue uninterrupted after hours of trekking through the night. Musicians set up in one corner. A golden throne, illuminated by four naked slaves with flaming torches, was set up, dangerously close to the edge. Himself the Divinity leaped from his chariot and was carried to his seat of honor, another slave carrying the kithara on a cushion woven with rose-colored silk and spun gold threads.

A lower throne accommodated the now Divine Poppaea Sabina, who sat, Hercules on a leash at her feet, being fanned by no less a personage than Pythagoras, whom I had once seen getting married to, and publicly consummating that marriage with, Himself the Divinity in a wig and wedding dress. Poppaea, it seemed, superseded all previous unions, of either gender.

Now came Tigellinus, the all-powerful right-hand man, with a contingent of Praetorians. They arrayed themselves in lines to protect the Emperor and the guests.

If I had hoped that our group would cower in the background, I hoped in vain. The Emperor beckoned for the gang of poets to sit upon the closest couches and though I tried to avoid his gaze, I could not avoid that of Herself, who summoned me with a crooked finger.

I took my place at the feet of my former master, now patron.

He whispered to me to come closer and I knelt, nestling next to his toga. "Welcome, Gaius Petronius Gaii Libertus Sporus," he said, and I heard my post-*manumissio* name uttered for the first time. Did I feel any different? Hardly. My dominus was my dominus. I did not think the bond could be severed, unless one of us should die.

Once enough wine had been poured, and enough tidbits had been set out, Himself, the Divine Nero Claudius Caesar Augustus Germanicus, Fifth God to rule the Eternal City, stood, and struck a few notes, tuning his instrument. He cleared his throat.

No one touched any tidbits.

He stood practically at the very ledge. Below, the city was in flames, as far as the eye could see. In the distance, the slums. Of course! The wooden structures, squeezed together, were tinder; the suburra was always burning. But the fire was creeping closer. More than the anticipation of the Divinity's performance was the gnawing dread we all felt.

First, he spoke. "Rome," he said, "is like the phoenix, flaming as it traverses the vault of heaven, ever created anew in the fire of death and rebirth. My ancestor, Aeneas, son of Venus, fled from the fires of Troy, bearing his aged father on his back, to found a new Rome in the heart of Latium. But I do not flee the flames. I race toward them, open-winged, bearing in my arms not an aging parent, but the entire people of Rome … *Rome* … not withered, paraplegic Anchises, but the beautiful youth Ganymede, another Trojan Prince, another of my venerable, ancient lineage, my great, great, many times great-uncle … he has come to life in the arms of Jupiter, awakened to godhood by my holy seed. For tonight, I am every one of my ancestors. Tonight, I am all the gods. Rome, like Minerva, shall burst fully armed from my head, filled with wisdom, grace, and ultimate truth. Do not think I am mixing my metaphors, children! All things are one. All the universe is one. All paths lead to me. I am the past and the future, and I am the eternal present."

"He's gone mad," my *patronus* whispered, for my ears alone.

Himself continued: "I shall sing of the dawn of the world. Of the age of bronze, when men were heroes and there were no modern weapons of fire-quenched Seric steel … no weapons that could rain down destruction on whole cities as there are in our modern times, the Eighth Century since the founding of Rome, a millennium since the Fall of Ilium."

But I could not measure time in millennia. I was still a boy, though I had lived a lifetime of sorrow already. I did not really understand the words. They spoke of myths and realities beyond my limited existence, and I only felt their import, not their meaning.

Above, the bright stars shone.

The Emperor began to sing.

You must understand … I have said this many times … that in those days, the Emperor was beautiful. His eyes were captivating. The jowls, the jagged furrows that came from his later insecurity about his own divinity, from his constant fear of plots and assassinations, they were not there. In that moment, he was the empire's idol, the golden child who had come to sweep away the parsimonious fussiness of the old cuckold Claudius, the insanity of Caligula, the moral depravity of Tiberius, and the severity of Augustus. He was the new world.

He sang of the flames, as he stood above the flames.

His was not a trained voice. His Greek was quaint, antiquated, and I did not really understand much of the Aeolic tongue, the dialect for lyric poetry. But when he sang, he *was* Cassandra, wailing in vain at her unbelieved prophecy, he *was* Hecuba, weeping as she mourned her fifty sons, he *was* the faithful Andromache, being carried off to be raped by Neoptolemus, a mere boy, fired by revenge and bloodlust. These ancient women were real to him … and he made them real to us.

I did not need to understand the words. This man, who owned the world, sang to me of the things I had experienced myself … the burning of my village … the enslavement … the chains … the violations … the hopelessness. Surely, I was as innocent as they come, for it seemed that he sang to me, that he knew my ache, my pain.

Nero's song blended with the keening of the wind. The distant crash of collapsing buildings were the drumbeats … no, the heartbeats. At this distance, a hundred thousand screams blended into a soft drone, a sympathetic vibration that cradled his arching melismas and spun his voice into a celestial fabric … the substance of the universe itself.

Did anyone else hear what I heard, see what I saw? I could not tell. My eyes and ears were for him alone. I felt suspended in time.

Then, the wind shifted.

Smoke was billowing around us. An acrid stench, like charred flesh and incense and offal all at once, seeped into the air, poisoning the smell of wine and fine viands. The fire was creeping towards the Palatine. Slowly, inexorably. We stood in a haze that was glowing … searing.

And still he sang.

But the people around us were panicking. They could not go anywhere or risk the Emperor's wrath, but they feared for their lives.

And still the Divinity sang, and still I watched him,

barely seeing the growing chaos around me.

The wind was stronger now, blowing smoke about the veranda, making it curl around the Corinthian columns of the portico behind us, making the audience cough, the slaves' arms unsteady as they tried to hold up their torches. One of the torch-women collapsed from the smoke. One of the Praetorians casually kicked her off the ledge. Sickness could not be allowed to mar the perfection of the Divinity's vision.

At last, the sound ended. But I went on staring at him.

A thought surfaced unbidden in my mind. A hopeless dream. A crazy joy that was as dark as the deepest despair. *I must have him,* I thought.

Around me I heard voices. "We can't leave this balcony. We can't go anywhere. We're completely surrounded by fire. We are trapped here until they put it out."

More wine was being poured. If people were indeed trapped, they were all going to drink themselves into a stupor. The building behind us, no doubt, had toilets, though probably no running water, as the aqueduct was probably being diverted to douse the fire. There was enough food in the banquet to last for days. But how many days would it take for the flames to die?

In one corner, some of the guests were already making love right there in the open. What else was there to do? Who knew whether the fire would reach the very summit of the Palatine?

Slowly, Himself the Divinity sat back down on his throne.

You see, I did not seduce the Emperor with my wiles. Only an overpainted whore like you would think in those terms.

On that day, Himself, the Divine Nero Claudius Caesar Augustus Germanicus, was still the best to have ascended the throne since the Julio-Claudians wrested control of the known world from the Senate, and reduced the Republic to a rabble of frightened yes-men. He was handsome. He was a poet, a singer, an actor — to be sure, this was hardly palatable to the sober patricians, for they were professions more proper to the Greeks, who despite having given Rome all its culture were still at root an enslaved race — but these things made him beloved of the people. He was generous. He had become Emperor at the age of only sixteen. He had begun his reign by promising to end corruption and to listen to the Senate. He had tried to abolish taxes completely — when that failed, he had regulated taxes and established stricter supervision. He had passed a law allowing slaves to protest their treatment to the local magistrate. Indeed, he had his deviant proclivities, but who in Rome did not? The people loved a bit of scandal. They loved that his love life played out in the public arena, an entertainment for the masses as absorbing as gladiatorial combat, chariot, or *damnatio ad bestias.*

On the day Rome burned, he was still only twenty-five.

The aura of the years when he had ruled with moderation and justice still clung to him. And he was beautiful, beardless, slender. He was godlike.

But that night, when he sang, the sublimity of his music, the splendid cadence of his words, did not put out the flames.

Instead, the gods willed that the flames turn towards the Palatine, threatening to consume even him. He had not commanded the wind and the flames.

In that moment, deep inside, I think he must have known for the first time that, though he was godlike, he was not a god. That must have been a terrible discovery for him.

So terrible it propelled his downward slide into depravity and darkness.

Yet in that moment, who was I to know anything?

In that moment, in my first day of freedom, I was made a slave again. In that moment, with all the volcanic passion that only an adolescent can feel, utterly, unconditionally, recklessly, and stupidly, I was in love.

XXII

NYMPHIDIUS SABINUS

As the fire consumed the night, there was nothing to drink but wine, and no water with which to dilute it. The heat … the wine … I must have dozed off.

And when I slept I had strange dreams. Borne by the wind, floating over the flames of Troy, sheltered from the fiery sun by the sheltering wings of a giant eagle. In my dream I was Ganymede and my abductor was the God of Love.

When I awoke, it was dawn. The July sun was barely up, but it beat down. Himself the Divinity's throne was unoccupied, and some guests appeared to have managed to slip away in his absence.

Below us, the fire raged, unabated; though some areas were completely gutted, others were flaring up anew. There did now seem to be a few possible pathways down from our vantage point, one of them more or less the way we came; another, more steep, led through what seemed to be a completely burnt-out sector of the city. The chorus of screams that had underscored the Emperor's ode had softened … now it was barely a whisper in the wind. But I knew people were still dying.

I had fallen asleep at the feet of my patronus, my head against his knee. At first I was conscious only of the heat … the harsh sunlight, the blast from the burning city. It looked like about the third hour, for the sun had not even reached its zenith, and already we were soaked in sweat. I forced myself to stand and looked around. Many of the aristocrats had already divested themselves of their clothing and some were rubbing themselves down with the melted snow from the troughs where snails and oysters had been chilled the previous night.

Now, some of the Praetorians were walking about, prodding and poking. One of them pulled the head of Octavia from a platter of pork. He and his friends were laughing. Another soldier, with a comical display of discretion, wrapped it in a military cloak and secreted in a nearby wine jar.

As noon approached, Himself and the Empress emerged onto the portico of the building behind us. I gasped. Somehow, amid the chaos, the Divinity had managed to spend time in the bath. He had been oiled and perfumed and wore only a cloak, fastened with a bronze fibula in the shape of a phallus. The fabric was only perfunctorily wrapped about the imperial torso. And I was still in love, so my feelings last night were not some delirium brought on by wine.

A soldier presented the Empress with yesterday's gift. She peeked into the amphora and seemed disgusted by the smell. She waved it away.

The Emperor made his way to his throne and she followed. He waved his hand and the guests fell silent.

"You may all go home," he said. "Those of you who still

have homes, that is. If you can find a way off this hilltop. You may all go home … *except …"*

Behind him came the terrifying Praefectus of the Praetorians, Tigellinus and his co-praefectus, Nymphidius.

Tigellinus said — he had a gravelly, unpleasant voice — "Senators and military officers to remain."

"Yes," Nero said. "We will have to make some logistical plans to ease the city's agony. We will need the senators and soldiers. Experienced heads and all that. And military discipline. Tigellinus, you must organize the vigiles to put out the fires."

"Easier said than done, Divinitas," said the praefectus. "There aren't enough vigiles. It is impossible to divert the aqueducts. There is a simple solution, but many will not like it."

"What might that be, Tigellinus?" said the Lady Poppaea, with the kind of sweet smile that makes men shrivel with dread. But not Tigellinus.

"Any neighborhood that cannot be saved," Tigellinus said, "we just burn the rest of it down. A good clean ending. The burning will stop when there is nothing left to burn."

"Yes, yes," Nero said. "Swift and clean. Like a surgeon."

Those who overheard this immediately began talking amongst themselves. Even though I could not take my eyes off the Emperor, I heard my master whisper, "This won't look good."

"I should send everyone else away," Tigellinus said. "In particular the artists, as their delicate sensibilities may balk at some of what must be discussed."

"Yes," said Himself. "Tell them, Tigellinus."

Tigellinus beckoned; Nymphidius came to his side. And

presently it was Nymphidius who was dispatched to give the order to disperse.

Good, I thought. *My patronus and I can go and see if anything remains of our home.* Petronius's mansion with its beautiful sculptures, its priceless vases ... I shuddered, trying not to think of all that my former dominus might have lost. I saw Croesus hovering about, gathering up Petronius's things. I looked across the valley. The fire was not dying down.

This Nymphidius — he theoretically shared the praefectus position with Tigellinus, yet always seemed to be the trained bulldog, not the mastermind — strutted officiously among the somewhat depleted ranks of dinner guests. He stopped here and there to pick at a tidbit here and there — a honeyed mouse embryo, a peacock's brain on a stick. He acted as if he owned the place. And wherever he thrust himself, people stepped back. He was not liked.

At length he returned to where I and my patronus were gathering our belongings. Nearby were the likes of Lucan and Seneca ... all the literary circle of Himself the Divinity. He saw that we were preparing to depart and he peered at all of us. On my former master, on the poets — the handsome young one and the dour one ... and last, at me.

"Everyone must leave the banquet now, unless you're a senator or a military officer," he said. "Do as I say, in the name of my ancestors!"

"His ancestors?" I heard someone whisper.

"He's a freedwoman's child, who fancies his mother was raped by Caligula," someone replied.

I do not know if Nymphidius heard. His eyes reflected nothing.

Not content to just leave, it was the poet Lucan who said, "We're all poets here."

"Literature, eh?" he said. "But the Divinitas is rather fond of literature, is he not?"

But he was not looking at the poets. He was gazing at me. And the *way* he was staring at me chilled me. Not that I wasn't used to being stared at. I was used to being mentally undressed, being the object of someone's random fantasies. Often, when I had been put on display by my master, I was not dressed at all, and I had been told so often that I was beautiful that it had no meaning for me.

So when a man or woman disrobed me with their eyes, I thought little of it. But Gaius Nymphidius Sabinus was not disrobing. He was disembowelling. His look made my skin crawl. I looked away.

Presently, I heard him speak again. "The Divinity has now informed me that literary figures, and their entourages, will remain as well. This coming time will not just be a time for dealing with a catastrophe. There will be a need for feeding the hungry and housing the homeless. But —"

"Well said, Nymphidius," came the voice of Himself. He was so close I could have reached out to touch him. I smelled his perfume. Between being aroused by the heady fragrance, and recoiling from the Praefectus, I was, to say the least, confused. "But," said the Emperor, "as you so rightly point out, we most deal not only with practicalities, but aesthetics. That's why I need my artists as well."

"This means you," said Nymphidius, apparently to the entire ensemble of poets. But his eyes were only on me.

And mine were only on the Emperor.

XXIII

AVERNUS

So you're telling me that this icon of debauchery and cruelty was actually some kind of paragon, a ... excuse the expression ... a God?

Wait! You're leaping ahead, and vapid as the rest of them, you've already forgotten that the Infamous One was once the most popular of Emperors. And if Himself were still on the throne, would you be getting me ready for a spectacular death, a mythic reenactment to entertain the feckless mob?

True enough. Still, you had a good run.

And a short one.

You've had enough happen in your life for someone four times your age.

Yes. Soon, I will be twenty years old.

The Fates have had your thread pinched off from the time you were born. I don't think you will elude it. So you might as well look as beautiful as possible. Hold still. You smudged your kohl.

From weeping, remembering the moment when I was an innocent, and innocently in love.

Come. The mob, as you call them, must be able to see the

beauty of the goddess from the topmost tier of the Circus Maximus. Once glance from your divine eyes must be enough to still their mutterings.

On the second day of the blaze, having dismissed most of the banqueters and hangers-on, nothing much was done. Himself merely sat, surveying the spectacle, and now and then receiving ever-more alarming reports of the damage.

Now and then he paused to sing a little, accompanying himself. All the songs he sang were tragic, but the most plangent was Niobe, mourning the loss of her children. Fourteen strophes and fourteen antistrophes, one of each for each of her slain sons and daughters; he outdid even the first night's performance about the Fall of Troy. When he sang, all conversation was naturally silenced — this was not merely from politeness, but also fear, for Nero's cruelest guard dogs stood ready to punish the slightest discourtesy.

We were hungry. Even the palace was running out of supplies. We were dirty and scruffy — for only the Emperor and Empress had been able to bathe. The communal lavatory had a queue and exuded a stench that could not even be masked by a liberal fumigation of frankincense pilfered from the imperial altar.

On the third day, Himself decided that we should all descend the hill and inspect for ourselves the scale of the disaster. "Money!" he cried. "Bring treasure chests and jugs and amphorae! Hunt through the trunks for trinkets. Aurei and denarii only — no bronze!"

A flurry of activity, in and out of the building behind us. I had not seen that much money in my life. I think that perhaps even the wealthiest in the gathering had not. The Emperor's concept of a *trinket* could pay the rent on a room in the suburra for a year or two.

I roused myself, knowing that we would finally be able to see what had become of the real world.

Himself summoned Tigellinus to him and whispered a few words. The praefectus barked out a new command. "By the gracious will of the Divinitas," he said, "you shall all enter the private caldarium within. He makes his *sanctum sanctorum* available for you mortals."

Himself the Divinity said, "Yes, indeed. It won't do at all for a manifestation from High Olympus to appear like a bevy of bedraggled dinner guests. We must pull ourselves together."

"Indeed," Lucan said, obsequiously falling to his knees, "you shall appear from the sky as redeemer of the world, personally hauling the plebeians back up from the gaping maw of Avernus."

"With the Divine Poppaea, indeed, as redemptrix," the Emperor remarked, without even a twinge of irony.

Petronius whispered to me, "I don't think I've ever heard a mythological allusion so mangled and abused."

Tigellinus said: "Right then! Groups of twenty! Disrobe quickly! The caldarium is inside, to the left, just past the public shitting chamber! No amorous activities please, Himself is in a hurry. And don't piss in the water. There are jars for that and the imperial laundry will be collecting."

We were all disrobing right there on the balcony: masters and attendants, slaves and millionaires, for the Romans are obsessed with bathing, and we were all caked with sweat, dried sauces, old wine, and vomit. The guests fairly charged into the building atop the hill which was little more than a private shelter for the Emperor or a few guests who would climb all this way for the view; it was not equipped for Imperial banquets.

When I and my master followed the guests to the building, Nymphidius stopped me as Petronius ascended the steps. Petronius turned and said, "Our group is fewer than twenty."

"He will go when I say," Nymphidius said. He laid a gnarled hand on my shoulder. You must realize what a state I was in. He was a Praetorian, a *chief* among Praetorians. I could suddenly feel a warm spurt between my legs. I was shaking. I was naked and I was terrified.

"Waste of good piss," Nymphidius said. "You know there's a fine for that."

And then he took me by both shoulders and pushed me up the steps.

The caldarium was already crammed; the command for "groups of twenty" had been ineffective, as people were so desperate to feel cleansed with warm water that they had rushed into the pool, not even bothering to scrape off the accumulated detritus of what was now a three-day party … three days and counting. Nor was the water hot. It was closer to a tepidarium.

"What are you waiting for?"

I turned and saw that Nymphidius was completely naked, save, perversely, for his helmet. He shoved me into the water and plunged in after. I became self-conscious. Everyone was watching me. Everyone from senator to cupbearer. And no one more than Nymphidius Sabinus, who stood so close to me I could feel him, ramming into my side like a truncheon, his eyes boring into me. I was terrified. But I dared not show fear now. I stared right back at him and saw insensate, insatiable hunger in his eyes. This was a man for whom nothing could ever be enough.

A foul-smelling steam enveloped us. Panicking, I considered climbing out of the pool. Then I caught a glimpse of Petronius, not far from me, the way blocked by a mass of overfed nobility. I elbowed my way through, and heedless of propriety and my lowly position, I clung to him fiercely, as tightly as if were in his bed, having a nightmare.

I could hear Nymphidius cackling like a malevolent fishwife.

"Sporus," said Petronius, "Remember you're a freedman now."

"I don't want to be free," I whispered.

"Yes, my Giton," he said, "you do."

"That man ... why does he frighten me so much?"

"You have an instinct, that's why. You know bad men right away. You don't know this, but I observe you sometimes, in order to pick out the bad apples in my own orchard."

"This place — it's like Avernus, the lake of noxious fumes, the gateway to the country of the dead," I said, remembering when he had read to me from Virgil, the part when Aeneas visits his departed comrades.

"We'll be home soon," Petronius said.

"If we even have a home," I said. "All those beautiful things ... gone, perhaps."

"Does it matter? I'll buy more," said my patron. "But I'll never be able to buy another Sporus."

At that moment, a consort of tubae and bucinae sounded

and Himself entered the chamber. A dozen slaves carried armfuls of tunicae, some purple-bordered togas for the senators, stolae in bright colors.

The Emperor announced, "Some new clothes to replace the shabby vestments you've just cast off. If I am going scatter all sorts of treats to the mob, I might as well make sure my nobles look the part. Jupiter and Juno need a proper entourage of Olympians, not a ragtag band of dissolute voluptuaries." He surveyed our group. Hercules, strutting behind Poppaea, his leash barely controllable by a frightened little Nubian, growled. Nero said, "There seem to be fewer of you than I had hoped. Tigellinus, did not the senators, the military, and the poets all remain behind?"

"Yes, Divinity. So I instructed."

"If anyone has slipped away, contrary to my direct order, make sure that the blasphemy is appropriately dealt with."

"What fun," Nymphidius smirked. "Perhaps my new little friend would like a front row seat at the proceedings?"

For he had sidled back up to me, and was endeavoring to slide a stubby finger into my posterior. I squirmed and clung to my former master even more tightly. Quicky, I climbed out of the caldarium and allowed a slave to wrap a toga praetexta about my shoulders. It was a woolen garment, and warm, too warm. A freeborn youth, a Roman citizen, who has not yet attained his majority, is privileged to wear the purple stripe. It was far above my station.

"… But you wear it well." Petronius had read my thoughts. "It suits you. You'll soon get used to the different way your two arms feel, the one encumbered, the other free to gesticulate."

We were assembling on the portico. I tried to stay out of Nymphidius's sight. Flute players began a keening, erotic melody, weaving in and out above the beat of a small drum. Nude boys sang and girls strewed flowers as the procession began. The heat, trapped in the valley, burned our faces; and it had been but minutes since we had bathed.

My master whispered to me, "Himself believes Himself to be the God, descending from lofty Olympus to redeem the city from its fiery apocalypse. He is arrogant. He is narcissistic. And yet, he needs their love. He is hungry for love. He consumes it, indiscriminately, thoughtlessly. But what will he give back? O Sporus, I've seen the way you look at him. He has charisma. A dangerous charisma. But Sporus, my beautiful child, do not love a god. You will be incinerated."

I wondered whether my lord and master, who had given me the gift of being able to see beauty, who had saved me at some risk to his own self ... whether he might not be a little jealous.

"You gave me freedom," I said.

"Yes, and now you are free to choose a long, productive old age, or to go down like Icarus, like Phaëton, flying too close to the sun."

The toga felt unnaturally warm. I was already beginning to sweat.

"We will have to see that you can be granted citizenship," Petronius said. "You will wear that garment without feeling lost inside it You'll go further if I can get the Emperor to grant you *civitas*. But he'll have to have you in his field of vision."

A foul wind sprang up.   The stench from the bath chamber filled the air, mingled with the incense they had been burning to hide the odor, and blending with the smell of charring wood and flesh that was carried upward on the wind. We started down the portico steps, toward the steep pathway that led down the hill.

"You said," my patron said, "that the bath was like Avernus, the stinking lake that leads to the underworld. Be prepared, my son. The place we are going to now is like the place beyond Avernus. It is hell itself."

I followed. I was filled with dread. There was going to be death down there.   Destruction on an unimaginable scale. And yet there was something else, a glimmer of joy. That was what I tried to think of as we descended to darkness.

Petronius had called me his son.

XXIV
SCAPEGOAT

It was, indeed, a descent into Hades. Our convoy, freshly bathed, dressed in gaudy clothes, perfumed, followed the Emperor's litter down the steep, narrow path … down toward where the flames were raging still.

Some of the party had whited their faces and rouged their cheeks. As we reached the upper circle of the infernum, the lead paint of their faces glowed with reflected fire. The first flat area we reached had been burnt out, though in the middle distance, there were more flames. Further off still, the fire was still burning strongly. Screams echoed from every side. The clearing was jammed with people. Some were dead and charred, some half burned, others sitting, dazed, or crawling about. The delegation from heaven halted, and Himself got out of his litter; a small rug was laid out on the ashes, and a curule produced for him to sit on.

The apparition of a glittering, bejewelled Imperial court in the midst of this vista of destruction and misery did not provoke immediate adulation, though I am sure Himself the Divinity expected nothing less. The sight was fantastical and jarring. Overwhelming, all the suffering — the crying babies, the groaning wounded. Dead and dying people everywhere. Charred severed limbs. Crawling, barely recognizable as human, those of Emperor's subjects who still lived were more animal than human, and the divine visitation was so far outside their realm of pain that we seemed to belong to a different reality altogether.

The Divinitas cleared his throat. No one acknowledged him. At length, he clapped his hands for the band to play a fanfare. Petronius and I, the whole poets' group, crept further down, and now we were seated right behind the throne. I could hear everything that was said. The Lady Poppaea turned and winked at me. Tigellinus and Nymphidius stood on either side of the Emperor. Dancers moved, awkwardly avoiding piles of ash.

Nero raised his hand and the musicians gurgled to a halt. "My children," he said, "I, the God, have heard your cries. I have descended from on high to bring you solace. Attend to my words!"

Then he called for his kithara, plucked a few notes, cleared his throat again, and began to sing. It was a song of unspeakable anguish, Hecuba lamenting over the ashes of Troy. As his voice had soared over the burning city below, now it blended with the shrieks of the dying.

Yes. It was beautiful. But my heart was sinking. This could not possibly be what Rome needed at this moment.

Surely the Divinitas could not know ... could not understand ... real suffering. I remembered my own village burning. The forced march to the sea. The chains. The beatings, the pirate captain "breaking me in." What could the Divinitas be thinking? These people had lost *everything*. There were not ghosts from Homer and Virgil.

There are times when a song cannot salve the heart.

Nero's public was not moved. Even he could see that, used as he was to constant fawning. He paused and beckoned to the Praetorians, and then he went on singing. Soldiers came forward with bags full of gold. They began tossing them into the throng. You would expect them to become like hungry wolves, diving for the gold, but this provoked little reaction. I saw a toddler reach out to pick up a coin, but its mother snatched back his hand; the aureus had fallen into hot ash.

Hesitantly, one of the wounded took a coin. Others turned to scold him. What was the problem? The Emperor went on singing.

Andromache mourning the death of the great Hector at the hand of Achilles, wailing over her child Astyanax, his brains dashed out against the walls of Troy by Neoptolemus, Achilles's son … who would soon make her his concubine. Polyxena, sacrificed to assuage Achilles's hungry ghost. And through it all, preternaturally beautiful Helen, gliding through the desolation, untouched by it all. The performance should have wrung tears in any theater, but this was no theater.

Presently, Tigellinus grew tired of the audience's inattention. He pulled out a little quirt and started to lash the nearest in the crowd. "Don't you recognize your Emperor and God? Show some respect!" And he set a ring of Praetorians to protect the Emperor, all ready with swords and whips, to wring obeisance from them.

Cowed, they huddled in a pathetic mass prostration. Surely the Emperor must stop singing now! But he did not. He went to the very end of the song, and all the way the soldiers scattered gold and trinkets, and the plebeians, their eyes dead and desolate, did not pick them up.

Once Himself the Divinity finished singing, he handed his kithara to an attendant. I saw his face. The flash of anger, certainly. But there was something else in his eyes … it was haughtiness, it was disdain … but also … he had the look of a rejected lover who wonders what he did wrong. *The Emperor is vulnerable,* I thought. *And he's lonely.*

He addressed the crowd directly.

"People of Rome," he said. "I've seen your suffering. I have come down from my home in the clouds. I've brought gold. I've brought coins and precious stones and rare objects. I am Jupiter and you are the beautiful Danaë, drifting on a sea of destruction. I shall rain down on you in a shower of gold, as Jupiter did. See, see — the glittering power of my love for you! I shall lift all of you out of this degradation. Out of your terrible suffering will come a Rome of gold and marble … together we shall build Neropolis."

Neropolis! But *Rome* was the urbs aeterna, in its eighth century since it was built on this spot by Romulus and Remus.

I thought I heard someone whisper the word *hubris.* But maybe it was just the wind. Less than a thousand paces away, fire was still blazing.

A tiny voice spoke up. "We can't eat gold!"

"Who said that?" Tigellinus said. He motioned for the guard to find the speaker. They dragged her in, not gently. It was a little woman in a torn red tunic. The sheerness of the crimson fabric, the painted cheeks, the heavy kohl that lined her eyes, all betrayed her profession. The whores must be out in force. The guards thrust her down on the hot ground.

"Do you dare contradict the Divinitas?" he said, and slapped her a few times. Her nose was bloodied, but she was defiant. She got up off the ground and looked her Emperor in the eye.

"Divinitas," she said bitterly. "Give us bread. The granaries are in cinders. All the gold in the world won't feed us if there's nowhere to buy food."

"Yes," came another shout. "We need food."

"Food! Food!" others shouted. The guards used the lash, but they would not stop. "Bread! Bread!"

"My children! Do not be disheartened. I'll find you grain. We're putting out all the fires. We will rebuild."

"You're not putting out the fire," came another voice, an old man. "The vigiles are burning down *more* sectors of the city."

"What!"

"A necessity, Divinitas," said Tigellinus. "There are neighbourhoods that are best levelled to the ground. If we don't destroy them, a random wind could spread the fire all the way to the Palatine."

"To my house?" Nero cried.

My house, I thought. *As large as most cities, and as yet mostly untouched by the flames.*

"Your house!" said the prostitute. "You're burning our houses so you can rebuild your own?"

A collective gasp came from the crowd … and from our people, too. The woman had said the thing that must not be said. And the mob wasn't turning on her. In fact some of them took up her cry. "Arsonist! Incendiary!" And then people were saying other things. "You killed your mother! You killed your wife!"

"Shall I fetch the archers, Divinitas?" Tigellinus said.

"You don't need subjects like these."

Nero was dithering. "More deaths?"

Petronius spoke up. "Divinitas, half the city has perished in the fire already. What is an Emperor without subjects? You don't need more corpses today. You need —"

"Oh, you are so right, Gaius Petronius," said the Emperor. "Always you bring me to my senses. You are the only one who brings order to my chaotic existence. You calm the tempest in my soul."

Tigellinus said, "They are exaggerating, Divinitas. Our men have only torched a couple of districts. Mostly slums anyway."

"You may stop now, Tigellinus. No more destruction. Don't kill anyone. Except traitors, of course." For the woman who had defied the Emperor was already being hustled away by the guards.

"Perhaps you should show her clemency, Divinitas," Petronius said. "The mob is in an ugly mood. They could … turn against us."

"We have to give them something. They're calling *me* an arsonist — the father of the country, the one who labors without reward on their behalf! We must give them somewhere else to direct their anger."

"They don't need destruction — they need distraction," said the poet Lucan, and the Emperor let out a little giggle at his clever turn of phrase.

"Food, first of all," said Petronius.

"And if there's no food, then what?"

"Entertainment," Nymphidius said.

"Someone to blame," said Himself, and I could see that he meant that person must on no account be Himself.

"Find one quickly."

"A scapegoat," said Poppaea.

"Yes, yes. Tigellinus — those men who set fire to those slums — have them crucified."

"Oh, hardly, Divinitas," said Tigellinus. "You can't execute the very people who put you on the throne."

"Don't be impertinent, Tigellinus," said Poppaea, who obviously feared the Praetorians far less than her husband. "He was just joking. My Divine husband … Pontius Pilatus gave me an idea, when he was going on and on about his past glories at the banquet."

"That washed-up old windbag?"

"He told me of a group of people here in the city that nobody likes. Targeting them would deflect the mob's anger … and also supply endless fodder for our city's flagging entertainment sector. And no one will miss them. They're just another cult from the east."

"Poppaea … you are quite brilliant. What are they called, these convenient victims?"

"I'm not sure. But I see Pilatus skulking about over there. I'm sure he'll tell you all about it."

There was a glint in the Emperor's eye. As I looked at him, I realized that the passionate, unconditional love for Himself that I had been feeling a mere two days ago was already starting to fray. It was giving way to more complex feelings. For I still loved him, but I was also beginning to understand him.

That was one of the consequences of being free. I could see past whether someone would have me beaten, would violate me, or at best, not even see me in the room … I could see who people really were. I could see beyond my own state of being chattel. Two days ago I saw perfection.

Today I saw insecurity. All called him Divinitas, yet deep inside, he knew he was no god.

Falling in love, falling out of love … and I had not even exchanged two sentences with Himself, he who owned the known world.

XXV

Neropolis

Of the Christiani, or Chrestianoi, or whatever they were called, the less said the better; they were a reviled and radical sect, and if *someone* needed to be sacrificed for the preservation of Roman values and civilization, why not? Nobody actually *knew* any of these people. The day that Himself made the decision, no one could be found to disagree, and the Praetorians were immediately dispatched to make it so. But the scale of it … that was something we did not expect. Nor the speed with which it began.

For my patron and me, and for our household as a whole, it was far more pertinent that somehow, Petronius's home had survived.

The fire had burnt itself out less than a hundred paces from the edge of his home. Farther up the hill, the villas were more or less intact, but looking downhill, the street was a wasteland. A dog was worrying at the corpse of slave. An old woman in a torn stola crouched and wept in the shadow of a broken column.

"The gods must love you," I told Petronius, as the door

slave opened the front portal.

"It's you they love, Giton," said my patronus, "for my time will come quite soon."

"How can you say this?" I said.

As I was about to step inside, we heard the old woman, who had come up to the threshold and was screaming curses.

"Dead! Look around you! All dead! And your master is to blame!"

Petronius took an aureus from a pouch and handed it to her. Her eyes widened. "Control yourself, woman," he said. "We did not do this."

"The fire swept uphill all the way from the suburra," Croesus said. "It was the wind, the will of the gods."

She sputtered. "You are the favorite of Himself, the only God who matters — the Incendiary — and it was his Praetorians that flattened this house! Not the wind! They only spared your villa because you are Gaius Petronius Arbiter! The favorite of the Divinitas!"

"The *gods* do not love me," Petronius said to me. "You see it now, don't you? Only *one* god in particular, and he's fickle."

The old woman had been a slave in the villa two dwellings downhill. As the doomsayer of the morning, she was appropriately named Cassandra. She told us how Praetorians had come, not to put out the flames, but to level the house. Her dominus and domina being somewhat old-fashioned, and having no estates in the country to escape to, had killed themselves to avoid the embarrassment of a drop of social status. Most of their slaves had run off.

"Are there no heirs?" Petronius said.

"We don't know. But we don't want the state to take us."
That would have been a bleak prospect indeed.
Petronius said, "Speak to Croesus, my steward. In the
midst of this mayhem, perhaps we can shelter a few of you
until we know who you actually belong to."

"Domine!" she murmured and prostrated herself. "I can
cook, I can make healing potions, I can brew poisons...."

When we entered, Petronius immediately knelt to thank
the Lares and Penates that the house had been spared.
Unfortunately there was nothing to sacrifice but a leftover
dormouse, but he wrung its neck deftly and slit its throat,
splashing its meager blood on the altar.

An old slave brought water and washed our feet. We
walked into the atrium and Hylas was there. He burst into
tears when he saw us. "Oh, domine," he said, "you,
Sporus, you, master, alive!" He patted down a cushion
and placed it on a curule for Petronius to sit.

Behind him came my patronus's nephew, Marcus
Vinicius. He had a jug of wine and was pouring it into a
krater for Petronius. He had ridden ahead to see that our
household was in order. I noticed that armor was polished
and his crest freshly dyed. "It's true, uncle," he said
ruefully. "The guard destroyed as many houses as they
saved. They said it's to stop the flames spreading, but
there could be other plans. *Neropolis.*"

"City of Nero?" I said. "Where's that?"

"You're standing on it," said Marcus.

"What!" said Gaius Petronius.

"However the fire started," said Marcus Vinicius, "it
suits the Divinity's purpose well enough. Neropolis, like a
phoenix, rising from the ashes of Rome! A city all in gold

and marble."

"And the poor?" Petronius said. "They'll have gold and marble, too, I suppose?"

"I don't think Himself's plans have quite extended as far as the poor yet," said Marcus wryly.

We sat in the atrium and watched the sky as twilight turned to night. The wine had turned sour in the fire, and there was no water; the aqueducts were doubtless being diverted to help put out the flames.

"Our city has lasted for eight centuries," Petronius said. "From a mere village to master of the whole world, eight centuries. I am a Roman — though I was born in Massalia, in Southern Gaul, that too is Rome. Rome is the world, and it is *my* world. I intend to die in Rome, not in Neropolis."

And Petronius read to us, not the distraught and hysteria-filled ravings of the Divinitas, but another account of the fall of Troy, one by a truly great poet. "*Quisque suos patimur manes.* We are all haunted by our own ghosts; we suffer our own private hell," he said. "Virgil died half a century before I was born, but his truth still lives."

Presently Marcus Vinicius rose and left us; I heard him and some junior officers speaking in hushed tones as they went back into the street. I poured my patronus more wine.

The night never became truly dark, because the fire was not spent, not completely. The air had a tang of smoke and burning flesh. When our master had drifted to sleep, Hylas and I carried him to the cubiculum and put him in bed. We lay on either side of him and fell fast asleep like that, the three of us. When I woke, we were both nestled in his arms. The aristocrat, the freedman and the slave. All of

Rome, in one small room, an oasis in a flaming wasteland.

The fire lasted two more days. We stayed in the house. The bread had run out by then, as our kitchen did not hoard supplies; the master liked everything to be fresh. There was a little pork; it had been roasted before there was time for it to spoil. There wasn't even a dormouse left to eat, as it had been sacrificed on the first day.

On the third day, a messenger came to the door. The Emperor was once again commanding our attendance, and this entertainment came with tickets. An entire basket of clay *tesserae* for distribution to the household, each stamped with seat numbers, gradus and locus, according to rank; and two special ones, small marble disks, inscribed with the names of Marcus Petronius Arbiter … and C. Petronius Gaii Libertus Sporus.

They were for seats in the Imperial Box at the upcoming Ludi.

"Games?" Petronius shouted at the messenger; the boy quailed and prostrated himself all the way to the floor.

"Yes, my Lord."

"What about renewing the city?" said my patronus. But I already understood the Divinity's intent. Misery had gripped the city, and more than money, more than bread, the citizens needed distraction. Entertainment.

Every great undertaking among the Romans must begin in blood. Every pledge of love. Every auspicious new enterprise. Every building project.

Before he could build Neropolis, Nero need a sacrifice. And to make a new city rise from the ashes of the greatest city in the world, the sacrifice needed to be big.

XXVI
LUDI

Since it would not be proper to arrive *after* the Emperor, Petronius was forced to rise at an unnatural hour. For me, it was not a problem. A slave always wakes up before his master and I was not really used to freedom yet.

We had to spend some time picking the right clothes and painting our faces a little bit, though it would not do to be too ostentatious, lest the Emperor think we were trying to eclipse him. It was almost noon by the time we arrived at the Circus, but luckily the Divinitas was a late riser.

"Noon!" said Petronius, as our litter-bearers took us to where there was a certain secret passageway, which fed into a subterranean hall from which one could access the Imperial box directly by means of a narrow stairway. "Noon," said my patronus again, "how deadly."

For noon, as even I knew by now, is notoriously the most boring hour at any Ludi. It is when they execute criminals, so there is none of the art of gladiatorial combat, where, while death often occurs, the finer points are important, and appreciated by the audience.

"No finer points for the moment," said Petronius.

"Except ... let me tell you about these underground passageways which lead to a certain corridor ... the cryptoporticus ... all the way to the Palatine. This is where they killed Caligula, you know. They say he was addressing a troupe of actors, but I've heard a slightly more ignominious story ... that the Divinitas needed to get out quickly to take a crap. That's why he had so few attendants that day."

The underground chamber was cool but soon we were ascending into the bright sun. I had seen no Ludi in person but it's one of the things slaves gossip about — who's winning, who's losing, did you hear how Didimus switched from retiarius to secutor, did you see the mock naval battle, you'll never guess who caught the raffle ticket with the three free slaves, he was a slave himself and his dominus took the look — it's a subject for chatter because almost all gladiators are slaves. So it's a pathway to freedom ... though it's fraught with danger.

But all the gossip in the world could not have prepared me. The *smell* alone! Blood and sweat and animal shit, all clinging to the humid air, and the monstrous, ravening sound that only ten thousand people can make when they want someone to die.

The smell! You never get used to it. I've worked at the Games all my life, from the time I helped with watering the animals till the time they discovered my artistic talents.

The big cats are the worst. They're loners. They don't like to be crowded. Sometimes they fight each other as much as the venators. And sometimes they're bored and won't eat. I was told, in Africa, it's the lionesses that do all the hunting. But the mob does like to see the big manes ...

they're like a centurion's crest almost, an emblem of virility, of power.

And that day … they say there were more big cats than in the history of Rome. They say they emptied Africa for that spectacle.

Yes. They kicked up sand and the particles were gritty in the nostrils and rank with spoor. Today it is not so bad. They perfumed the entire arena, I see. No expense spared for my great and final drama. My death will be one of the costliest expenditures of the new régime.

When we arrived in the box, I kept blinking in the bright sun. Sweat started to pour down my face and the smell was intolerable, despite a brazier burning frankincense and two slaves sprinkling perfume. The Imperial throne was unoccupied, but armed guards stood at every corner of the box. More of a pavilion, really; it could have held a hundred guests, but currently there were only a few poets, whom I recognized, all grumbling because of their forced attendance. Not loudly, you understand. The Praetorians *might* not have understood. Though, to be honest, they were from Germania. They probably knew only basic Latin, and less Greek.

Petronius took a seat, not too close to the throne. I did not feel I merited an actual seat, being only a freedman, so I sat at his feet, as I had done so many other times. Apart from the poets, there was a senator or two, and the usual guards and slaves. A naked Nubian gymnast gyrated in a corner, unwatched.

It was Lucan who noticed me first, in fact. "Amazing to see you wearing clothes, for a change," he said.

"Sporus's days as a delicatus are over," Petronius said. "You're a bit behind on the news, aren't you? I manumitted him."

Lucan said, "Sorry. My house burned down. No time for gossip."

"I'm sure the Divinitas will build you a new one; just flatter him about his newest ode."

"Would you just look at that!" Seneca said, as a lioness strutted past the box with a baby in her jaws. "I know the Emperor means to be thorough, but who wants to see *that?*"

"Who wants to see *anyone* getting eaten?" said Lucan. "I'm waiting for the real show to start."

My eyes glazed over as I watched wave after wave of helpless people being driven onto the sand with whips and goads. There seemed to be an inexhaustible supply of Christians, and an equally endless array of cats. The cats were in no hurry. This wasn't a hungry pride chasing down an antelope.

"They're getting bloated," Lucan said. "Such gross mismanagement."

I was not happy to see Nymphidius enter the box next. He stalked about, glowering. Apparently the lions' feast was simply too boring. As one of the two chief Praetorians he was directly answerable to Himself.

"Why are there so *many* of them?" Lucan said. "Surely there's some kind of system to manage the ratio of cats to captives. You people are masters of these big spectacles."

Nymphidius growled, "But *these* people — they're crazy! The only requirement to avoid getting eaten alive is a one minute ceremony, pinch of incense, a one-sentence declaration of the Divinitas's divinity. When they hear and smell the lions, people will do *anything* to avoid being eaten — we were expecting at least a fifty person turnover

— and they're *all* going in to the arena! They're bewitched. It's exasperating."

"Surely," Petronius said, pointing to the half-eaten baby that one lioness was still worrying at, "that little thing wasn't expected to offer up the incense?"

"That's the horror of it," Nymphidius said. "They won't even let us take the babies. Afraid they won't be martyred. Worried they'll miss out on paradise."

"What a heartless cult," said Petronius.

"Indeed," said the Praetorian. "Imagine insisting on your children getting eaten along with you, just because you're too stubborn to say a few words to the Emperor's statue! These people aren't civilized, I tell you."

Nymphidius noticed me and stopped complaining for a moment. "Come here, boy, let's have a quickie behind the drapes."

"I'm *free*," I said.

"And I'm armed," he said.

I put my arms up, trying to ward him off.

At that moment, though, I heard a familiar growl. "Hercules!" I cried, as the Empress's cheetah tugged at the Praetorian's cloak. The guests in the box laughed. Nymphidius was not popular. Indeed he immediately straightened up and bowed to Poppaea Sabina, who had entered quite noiselessly.

"You bad boy!" she said, wagging a finger … not at me, I suddenly realized, but at Nymphidius, who was quivering like a plate of larks' tongues. "Sporus is not to be molested, you understand. He is my special guest, and under my protection. More importantly, he is under Hercules's."

"Divinitas," I murmured in relief. I wouldn't normally

have been pleased to see her, but she reined in the slobbering Nymphidius effectively. She beckoned me now to take Hercules from an old slave who was barely able to hang on to the leash. Hercules came willingly to me and nuzzled against my calves like a dog. Then, as the Empress sat down, she bade me sit at *her* feet while she played with my hair.

"We have a problem, Empress," said the Praetorian. "The cats won't eat."

"Then scourge them."

"Scourge who, Divinitas?"

"The Christians, you idiot. The lions are far too expensive."

Nymphidius ordered a few of his flunkies and they left the box. Presently, some burly, heavily armored soldiers started whipping the Christians, and they began swaying back and forth and stumbling toward the lions, who still didn't seem that interested.

Then, suddenly, they all started singing. It must have been some paean to their god. A few hundred people, their arms linked, singing an eerie, keening music. They rocked from side to side in time with their chanting. The audience started to pay attention. The Christians' chorus rose up in the sultry, stinking air.

Then there was a miracle, of sorts. The animals began to stir. Perhaps the music set off some primal hunger. They started to rush at the Christians, running them down, ripping throats, tearing off limbs. The crowd was howling and applauding. And still they sang. Some in the audience were impressed; they were even cheering them on.

"This is not a good look," said the Empress. "They're

supposed to be abject, miserable creatures, being crushed by the might and majesty of the city they tried to burn down. These look more like heroic figures."

"I'm glad the Emperor isn't here to see this débâcle," said Petronius. "He's planning to sing himself, and he doesn't like to be upstaged."

And then, after a blast from a consort of blaring bucinae, Himself was there. He stood at the entry from the cryptoporticus, resplendent in gold and purple, coming close enough to touch, while thousands rose and shouted his name, a thunder-roar that really set off the animals now. They were leaping on their prey, and the sound of crunching bones almost drowned out the singing. You could barely hear the hymn above all that racket.

Nero Claudius Caesar Augustus Germanicus took his seat. And I, my head in the lap of his Empress, was staring right into his eyes.

And he into mine.

XXVII

Mors et Amor

I was on the step, wedged between two thrones, and a living god was caressing my hair. I almost pissed myself. The line between the Divinitas's charm and his rage was easy to cross; even I knew that.

"Lovely, your hair," said Himself the Living God. "Not as silky as Poppaea's but ... muskier." He bent down and smelled the top of my head. No wonder Petronius had bade me be liberal with the perfume! "One of my favorite scents," he continued. "Remind me to have some more sent over to Petronius's."

Warily, I looked across to my former master.

"Lucius, dear," Poppaea said, ostentatiously addressing the living god by his praenomen, "the boy doesn't belong to Petronius anymore."

"Then we must acquire him," said Nero.

"Petronius told me he's been freed."

"No one is really free, where *my* will is concerned," said Nero. Without malice, just the truth. "Eleutheria thanatos."

"As you say, Divinitas. There is freedom only in death." I threw myself down at Himself's feet with an extravagantly obsequious move and kissed Himself's feet a few times. I think I missed the actual skin, though my teeth bumped against a ruby the size of a quail's egg. "I beg you, Divinitas, my Lord, my supreme God ... Petronius is finishing the *Satyricon* and he has made me his muse. I implore you, let me stay with him at least until his masterpiece is done."

"Brazen, aren't you?" said the Emperor. "I should have you thrown off the balcony. Your meat is probably sweeter than those sedition-mongers'." I thought my life was over, right then and there. Then he began to laugh uproariously.

"Don't, my dear," Poppaea said. "He's not ready for your malignant sense of humor yet."

"You should have seen the look on your face!" said the Emperor. Then he drew me up by the shoulders and kissed me on the lips.

Poppaea looked askance, but then she clapped her hands. The whole court followed suit. The Emperor let go and I slumped back down onto the steps in front of the throne, unsure about whether I should slink away to the relative safety of Petronius.

The Emperor waved for my patronus to approach.

"You've found a good muse," he said. "Although he's quite impertinent. He's been free for all of ... a week? and already so forward with his betters?"

Petronius said, "Ah, but before the pirates captured him ... he was a prince."

The Divinitas nodded. "That would explain it."

I looked at Petronius, a bit panic-stricken. After all, Petronius *knew* I was just some village ragamuffin. Or had

Aristarchos revealed the "origin story" he had concocted while training me in how to behave amongst aristocrats? Petronius's face betrayed no mendacity at all, but he was an accomplished courtier, suave when he flattered, lying with a smile.

The Emperor said to me, "So, Sporus, what kingdom did your father rule? Do you think I should conquer it? Are there more beautiful people there for me to own?"

Petronius said, "I'm not sure it would be worth it, Divinitas. I think it's barely more than a village. I doubt Sporus could find it on a map."

"Let the boy speak for himself."

"It's true, Divinitas. I hardly remember it."

"Perhaps my Germans would know. Do you speak their language?"

"Their language has some similarities to that of my people," I said, "but I don't really understand it. In Rome I've met only a few people who know my speech."

"Are you Dacian? Macedonian? Those places are all mine already, you know."

"No, Divinitas. Well, where I lived, we didn't really know about Rome. Our ... kingdom was very ... inward-looking."

"Not know about Rome?" The Emperor was genuinely mystified at this. "Now I *really* want your kingdom. Are there such places left in the world?"

I didn't want a Roman legion descending on what was left of my village. Not that I could actually lead the way there. I improvised. "Don't waste your valuable men, Divinitas. I'm a prince, and they killed my father. I may well be all that's left of my people. If you possess me, you already possess my country."

"You are as witty as you are beautiful," said Himself. I admired him then — yes, I had been in and out of love with him before even exchanging two sentences, and I am told that this is what is like to be young — but can you really be surprised that he could turn a boy's head just like that? Wealth and power and looks — are those not the three most alluring characteristics of a lover? He had all three. The first two in greater abundance than any other human being, and as for looks ... he was young. He was adored. He had the voice of an angel. And I must say this as well ... every man who had ever forced himself on me had had an unpleasant smell. Even Petronius, who never took advantage of me at all even though he had every right to ... he had a faint odor behind the layer of expensive perfume.

And the living god smelled like orange peel and cloves. Like the summer sky. Even here, in the stench of blood and guts and sweat and incense ... he was an island of freshness in a cloud of decay.

And, like a thoughtless child, I just sat on the step and stared up into his eyes.

"Divinity ... Divinity ..." Nymphidius said.

"What?"

"The executions are going ... rather slowly. The lions should have been done by the time you arrived, so we could get on to the more intellectual shows. But our guests of honour have made a mess of things. They all refused the incense, so they *all* have to get eaten."

"Quite the cult," said the Emperor.

The crowd had quieted down after its frenzy of greeting the Emperor. There was a lull in the arena. The animals prowled to and fro, no longer interested in their banquet.

Oh, a few of them worried at a severed limb. A few heads were being gnawed at. It was sickening yet strangely riveting. Most astounding of all was the seeming indifference of the throng. Though he was trying to stay calm, I could tell that Nymphidius was beside himself.

"We can't have all this dead air," said Nero. "They need to be entertained. When there's no bread, they *must* have a circus."

"Divinitas!" Nymphidius said. "We'll get through this lot as quick as we can."

"You'd better," said Nero. "The crowd will start to get sympathetic. You never know when they'll decide the criminals are underdogs."

Poppaea added, "That would be political suicide."

"Yes, of course, my dear," he said. To me he whispered, "You see. That's all my wife thinks of. And all I care about is my art. The world is the greatest canvas, and the only canvas appropriate to a God."

I had no answer to that. I only continued to gaze at him. He was only partly in our world. He also belonged to a more rarefied universe — the world of the gods, I supposed.

"Do you know who taught me to think like that?" he said. "Your master. Gaius, my arbiter of taste."

"He understands the universe, Divinitas."

"As do you, child," he said. I was falling in love all over again.

At that moment, however, the quiet in the Circus was shattered, much to everyone's relief. The Christians were now singing up a storm. As they sang their paean to their invisible god, the crowd became incensed, and they began chanting as well, a song in praise of the Olympians, from

Jove to Vulcan and not excluding a coda that extolled all the great God-Emperors of the Julio-Claudians (somehow they managed to skip Caligula.) The dueling chants were thrilling and then the music-master caused consorts of bucinae, tubae, water-organs, and tympani to play from opposite sides of the arena, melding into a blood-curdling cacophony. Slaves dropped flaming bales of straw behind the cats, to enrage them and to drive them further towards their prey.

Finally, the lions were aroused again. They roared — have you heard a hundred lions roar? — they sprang upon the Christians that remained and made quick work of them. The audience was jeering and hooting. The wind instruments were blaring. Each time someone's head was bitten off, the audience howled and laughed.

"Well, it seems to be working," said Nero.

The Empress clutched his hand. Rather, their hands clasped each other using my head as a cushion. The feeding frenzy went on and on, with fountains of blood, arms and legs being flung in every direction, beasts fighting each other over this corpse or that, but most terrifying of all was the noise of the crowd, their primal joy in bloodletting, thousands upon thousands of human beings howling above the din of the brass and the drums and the screams of the dying.

"I feel a song coming on," said the Emperor.

He called for a lyre.

As he stood, I was able to scamper away, because Himself had finally found something more interesting than me to focus on — Himself was now contemplating Himself. Or at least, his art.

He sang.

I crawled over to my former master.

"You flirted with him," said Petronius. "That is dangerous. It would have been better to just keep still and let him do whatever it is he plans to do to you. Passivity bores him, and it's better to bore Nero than to pique his interest."

The Emperor sang.

They were clearing the arena now. The beasts were being driven back to their cages which would descend through a system of hydraulics down to the labyrinth beneath the area. Those corpses not completely eaten were being drawn by hooks out through the Gates of Death.

The audience could not hear the Emperor; his song was for his private guests alone. More dignitaries were arriving now, well-dressed equites, aristocratic women with their hair piled high and with jewel-studded fibulae pinning their silk stolae. These were not all the literary circle that the Divinitas loved to have around him; there were politicians, military men, doddering old senators. Slaves poured wine and set out extra seats.

In the stands, too, the empty seats were filling up, for the noontime executions of criminals were often an excuse for lunch and a post-prandial nap, and now people were coming back, hoping that the afternoon's spectacles would be more engaging. There was another audience, as well, for the arena was being decorated with crosses, from each of which hung one of the alleged incendiaries. They were strung up only with rope — no nails — doubtless to prolong the excruciation, for otherwise they might have bled out in a few hours. No one paid much attention to them. The sight was so commonplace in Rome as to arouse no curiosity. They soon blended into the background.

More horn calls now, and heralds proclaiming the next tableau in the program...

A brief divertissement: a group of Chrestianoi who have been rooted out of our own armed forces will fight to the death against dwarfs mounted on ostrich chariots ....

A fresh batch of prisoners was being driven in by soldiers with whips. They were given wooden swords — a mockery of the meaning of the wooden sword, as it normally would signify that a gladiator has been given his freedom — and then came the ostrich chariots, each one driven by a full-sized charioteer, but manned by two pint-sized archers. The mob went wild! One of the victims actually managed to jump onto a chariot and despatched the dwarfs by braining them against the side of the car! The crowd demanded this one's freedom and he was allowed to slink out through the Gates of Life, demanding to be martyred a different way as he left and crying that he was a sinner and deserved death....

A reenactment of the Siege of Troy, complete with not one, not two, but SIX wooden horses! For your delight, the hapless citizens of Troy will be played by ... more of those traitorous Chrestianoi ... the ones who hate us ... the ones who burned your beloved city!

Fresh victims now filled the arena. And it went on and on. Hour after hour, and always ending in death. Then, as the sun began to set, something new. From the hydraulic platform there arose a vast, gleaming model of a city. Constructed in wood and painted white to simulate marble, the model had temples, palaces, even a new Circus. Conspicuously absent were any insulae for the poor.

Behold! cried the heralds. *From the ashes of the old, a*

Greater Rome rises. It shall be called, no longer Rome, but City of Nero!

"Why now?" I said to Petronius. "It will be dark soon." The crowd did not seem pleased.

I spoke too soon. At a signal from the Divinitas, the hundreds of crosses where Christians had hung all afternoon were set aflame, for they had been treated with pitch. The light transformed the model city. It seemed to come to life. It glowed. It gleamed in the light of people being burned alive. The crowd murmured, then burst into applause, shouting *"Neropolis! Neropolis!"*

"Marvellous!" exclaimed the Emperor. "But Nymphidius, I hope there are enough crosses left to burn at my garden party tonight."

Petronius looked at me. He drew me into a sad embrace. "Eight centuries," he said, "of the greatest civilization in the history of the world. Gone in an evening. Kiss me, my Giton. There won't be many more kisses. I don't plan to outlive Rome."

XXVIII

SACRIFICES

There were plenty of crosses for the garden party. That evening, though more than glutted with gore, we had to sit through another banquet, this one in the imperial gardens. But it was so crowded that we managed not to be seen.

Even some of the aristocrats were homeless for a while, and unable to get food in from their country estates, so the Emperor's largesse was welcome; the rich could still banquet while their slaves went hungry waiting for the next bread delivery.

It was difficult to enjoy the lavish offerings, because the screams of the flaming torches overwhelmed all conversation. Pilatus, the washed-up old general, was holding forth about the cult Rome loved to hate, though his only knowledge of them was from signing their founder's death warrant three decades ago … an incident he had probably forgotten, until it became a good dining out story.

I was surprised that we left the banquet early. My patronus was usually very careful, never dropping the slightest hint of anything negative towards Himself.

I was surprised, too, that Petronius went straight to bed before the sixth hour of the night, for usually this was the time when he was at his most creative. More often than not he would be scratching on a tablet or writing on a scroll at breakneck speed, sometimes asking me to sit quietly in a corner in flickering lamplight, "inspiration" he would call it.

But this time he went straight to the cubiculum, not seeming to notice whether I followed or not. Not wanting him to be alone, I crept in and saw that he had thrown himself on the bed without even removing his sweaty festive garments. He was already snoring lightly.

Quietly, I undressed and lay beside him, wondering how many more times we I would do so. But I, too, quickly fell asleep, my hand gently rubbing my patronus's belly.

I dreamed of dark things.

In my sleep, a lion pursued me through a dark arena. Above, distorted faces jeered.

In my sleep, I wore a crown of thorns and I was nailed to a cross, and it was being hoisted into the air … and strange people, dark-eyed, with guttural voices, mocked me in a strange language. *Queen of Hell*, they were calling me. Black petals streamed from the sky … and the earth parted, and a dark god stood in a sulphurous cleft, and he bellowed wind and thunder. The earth was shaking.

I woke.

No god thundered. But Petronius was gently moaning, with closed eyes. Above him, wedged between my lord's thighs, a naked Hylas rocked back and forth, pleasuring my patron. A lone lamp illumined Hylas's face. His eyes held a terrible melancholy. Hylas had mocked me when I first came, he seemed to know of nothing beyond the life of a pleasure-toy. And now he did his job, skillfully, feeling nothing.

Petronius was not even awake; Hylas had responded to some stirring in his master's sleep. Presently, my patron shuddered, convulsed, and groaned in release; then he fell still. Hylas calmly wiped off his still sleeping master and then he glanced over at me. When he looked at me, he saw I was awake, and he smiled.

And in that smile, he told me he loved me.

He eased himself off his master, and he lay down with Petronius between us. He never took his eyes off me.

"How long have you …" I whispered.

"Always."

"But you never said anything."

"Slave," he said softly. "Me not exist. But you … you became free, like real human being."

"What do you want from me?" I asked him.

"Nothing…."

"Except?"

"To go down the hill at dawn with you, make sacrifice at Apollo temple, swear me love you." I had thought him hardened; he had been ill-used since he could barely walk, I did not doubt. I wished I had learned more about where he came from, and what dark history he had endured before being saved by Petronius — for I did not doubt that every pleasure slave in my former master's home had somehow been saved from a far worse existence.

I do not know what I felt, really; I knew that if I said a cross word, he would be disconsolate. So I said, "All right, Hylas, I will go to the temple with you … because it is something you need … though unless my patronus frees you, your love is as much his property as your body."

Though we had had little sleep, we did go before dawn. We could not go far. Hylas did not really have permission to leave the villa but as a freedman I supposed I could vouch for him if asked. Hylas was both companion and link-boy, holding up a torch in the narrow dark street.

There was a small shrine at the foot of the hill, more closet than temple, really; it mostly catered to slaves. I had hardly looked at it when we passed by before, because I was usually in the litter with the dominus, and dared not peer through the curtains without his leave.

A woman sold doves at the entrance and Hylas bought a brace, paying for them himself with a worn sestertius. "Why waste your peculium?" I asked him. "I can pay."

"Me bring, me pay," Hylas said.

The room was dark. There was so much incense that you could not see the walls, so though the temple was tiny from the outside, it appeared infinite within. From somewhere beyond the chamber came the sound of a Greek double flute, wailing and undulating, like a couple in the throes of lovemaking.

The priest was a withered, tiny man who at first glance did not look as though he could ever have been in love. His voice was high and chirpy. He barely glanced at us. Another couple was leaving, an old man and a girl young enough to have been his granddaughter.

The priest spoke Greek, but with an exotic accent; he was not from one of the centers of the Hellenistic world like Egypt, but from some far corner of the empire. He said to us, "You have come here of your own free will, to declare your love?"

So far, no reason to lie.

The priest said, "You are in the presence of Apollo, who knows all truths. If you lie to each other, in this place, under the eye of the god, the god will curse you. You shall never find happiness together, and you shall never find happiness apart. Think about that before you say anything."

Beyond the smoke, in a shaft of light, we could see the face of the god. It was a crude, wooden statue, probably very ancient, not like the realistic marble in the temples of the rich. The paint was worn, but not the eyes. They had been retouched. The whites were blinding, precisely caught in the light beam. The irises were pale blue. The god stared down at us, his eyes unreadable. It was as if he meant to say to us, Truth is an absolute thing; there is no bending, no shading. And I was afraid; I had only come to humour Hylas, knowing that he would face a terrible future if he lost his dominus. Even if Petronius were to free him in his will, how would he live? In a brothel? And when lost his youth, would he be sitting at a desk selling tokens, making change for some whoremonger?

"Now," said the priest, "kill the birds."

We each took a dove and wrung its neck. We placed the birds on the altar.

"Close your eyes," said the priest. "Reach out and clasp each other's hands."

I felt Hylas's grip, cold, a little sweaty. The priest said, "Form an image of your beloved in your mind's eye. Say to that image all you have always wanted to say. Under the eye of Apollo Truthsayer, your words are blessed; and that which you dream, he can make real."

I tried to see Hylas's face in my mind but it was only a blur.

S.P. SOMTOW · 221

Hylas whispered, "Me Hylas, puer delicatus of dominus Petronius. Me swear. Me forever faithful to Sporus. Alone him me love."

An image began to form in my mind. I said to the image, "By Apollo Truthsayer, I declare: I am Gaius Petronius Gaii Libertus Sporus. I will live for you. I will die for you."

Fiercely, Hylas went on, "Me serve you. Me yours. For always."

And I said to the face that had vividly materialized in the darkness behind closed eyelids, "I will never betray you. I will protect you with my life."

The priest said, "Swear by the lives of the two white doves you have killed with your own hands. Their death stands as witness."

I tried to say more to Hylas, but I could not; the face that appeared unbidden to me was the face of Himself, the living god, the master of the world, the poet, the burner of cities, the singer of songs, the murderer of innocents.

We walked back arm in arm. I wondered whether what I had said constituted a lie for which I would be brutally punished. But I hadn't spoken to Hylas. Surely the god could see into my thoughts, could know that I intended no deception.

And yet I feared the curse. Because what do intentions matter?

Did Oedipus *intend* to kill his father and make love to his mother?

Fate, some say, is immutable.

As we arrived at the entrance, I saw the Lady Poppaea leaving in haste. Behind her, through the open door, I could see that the house was in an uproar. She had come with only a dozen guards, and she made them wait by the entrance. It was still not yet dawn.

Poppaea said to me, "Ah, already cheating on your patron with the slave boys!"

"My Lady —" What could I say to someone I had known so intimately, yet who now had the power to kill me with a single word … even a glance?

"You'd better hurry," she said. "I will see you again soon, sooner than you think." Ominous words.

The Empress climbed into the litter and drew the curtains. The soldiers and litter-bearers moved away quickly, the slaves trotting, the soldiers marching in double time. This was no official visit. It was as close to incognito as an Empress could get.

We entered the house. Things were being packed. I could see a cart being readied, a few valuables and clothes being loaded onto the back.

I saw Petronius, moving in the foyer, in a daze. He waved us away.

The steward said, "Quick. Pack. You know there's no carts in the streets after sunrise!"

"Where are we going?" I said.

"Cumae," said Croesus. "He means to consult the oracle."

Hylas stood in the doorway, confused, eyes flecked with terror.

"Shall I take Hylas?" I said.

"Take who you like," Croesus said, "only hurry. The Empress came to warn. Tigellinus has obtained a warrant for Petronius's arrest."

"But the dominus hasn't committed any crimes!"

"Treason, apparently."

"Treason? You mean, not staying for the end of the last banquet?"

"Who knows?" Croesus said.

"It must be a mistake."

I felt my patron's hands on my shoulders. I looked up at his face. If he had looked panicked before, it was gone now. His expression held a preternatural calm. He smiled at me. His eyes already seemed not of this world. They were like Apollo's eyes, penetrating my soul, peering from the fog of incense.

"Gods don't make mistakes," said Petronius Arbiter softly.

XXIX
SYBIL

It was the next morning before our party reached Cumae, travelling at a leisurely pace and stopping only for a brief prandium, and a change of horses, on an estate belonging to Marcus Vinicius, and then again for an equally brief cena at sunset, at some great lord's latifundium.

The journey was smooth and uneventful and for all the world like a household jaunt to the countryside … not the final journey of a man marked for treason. We sat in a covered cart, my patronus, Hylas, and me, and behind, in another, many of Petronius's favorite women; women of every hue, including the giantesses who had first taught me how to look beautiful.

They passed the time by singing songs and picking out ancient melodies on a kithara.

As I said, we left long before dawn, to avoid the interdiction on daytime wheeled traffic in the streets of Rome. Cumae is over a hundred *mille passuum* away from Rome, but our convoy made good time. The road was clear and straight and well kept up.

Cumae is older even than Rome. But the whole town is centered on only one thing, the Sybil.

So as we approached, people were already setting up roadside souvenir stalls, even an hour or two from the shrine, and there was an array of cauponae and tabernae to choose from, each more sordid-looking than the last. Croesus went to negotiate a room; we would likely not be spending the night, but I don't think my patronus intended to take the entire party down into the Sybil's cave. They would be able to spend the day shopping, or eating sweetmeats.

After settling the household in the upper story of a taberna that did not appear too filthy, Croesus had the dominus's litter brought down from the baggage cart, and bade the bearers straighten out their tunicae and do their hair. Gaius Petronius Arbiter was not just anyone, and he wasn't going to sneak up on the Sybil of Cumae.

I had the privilege of riding with Petronius. My former master did not seem at all perturbed by the fact that he had likely been condemned to death. Indeed, he acted as though he would live forever. And as we were carried toward the shrine, he wanted to make sure I knew all about where we were going.

"The Sybil," he said, "is a thousand years old ... older, even. She is so old that she has shrunk to the size of a cricket, and her voice is a squeaky stridulation."

He told me how Apollo loved her, how she had asked to live for as many years as the grains of sand she held in her fist ... but she had not asked for eternal youth, and that is why she has been withering away since before the founding of Rome. "I wrote of her in the *Satyricon*," he said, and reached for a scroll. He read to me, in that vivid way he had of telling a story, "… and I saw the Sybil with my own eyes, hanging in a bottle, and the boys were asking her, in Greek, what she desired: *Sibylla, ti theleis?* and she answered, *Apothanein thelo.*"

"I want to die," I repeated in Latin.

Did my patronus want to die?

"You're asking me with your eyes," said Petronius. "No need to say it aloud."

"Well, *do you,* my domine?"

"Don't call me that, I freed you."

I threw my arms around him. He daubed my eyes with a fold of his toga. "There, there," he said. "Look, how ironic … it's I who am comforting you, when you have so much still ahead of you."

But I was inconsolable. I was glad Hylas did not see me break down like this. As my patron held me hard to his chest, I felt the litter being lowered to the ground and one of the bearers was tugging at the curtain.

We were in a grove of some kind and there were stone steps leading down into a cavern. The steps were worn, each slab of stone with a smooth hollow from centuries of pilgrims' caligae. The litter-bearers waited above; everyone else was at the taberna, so my patron's penultimate act was something he wanted to share with me alone.

The steps descended into a cavern, and there were boys there, slaves of the oracle perhaps, whose job was to collect gifts, sell sacrificial animals, and assist the squeamish in those little commonplaces of worship, such as wringing doves' necks. They also controlled traffic to the inner caves and there was quite a system to it all; they had made it efficient, even mechanical, over the centuries. "It's all so orderly," my patronus said to me, "you could almost say that they've made a quintessentially Greek mystery into something quite Roman."

"I think that a shiny aureus will let us jump the queue," I said. I paid the boys myself — a minor fortune to be sure, but I loved Petronius.

"The power of coin! That, too, is very Roman," said Petronius. "Ah, the burden of Empire."

Impressed, the slave elbowed his way through the other supplicants and brought my master and me to a portal hewn from the rock, shaped like a tall isosceles triangle.

From within came a sound that really was like a cricket ... a lone cricket singing after winter has already come ... singing at the borderland of death. And the smell of incense, so powerful I was choking on it. "Be brave, my boy," said Petronius, and he took me by the hand.

We passed through one cave then another, following the boy who had taken my money. Each cave was entered through one of those triangular openings. The caves grew darker, the clouds of incense thicker. The voice of the cricket grew louder.

At length we reached what seemed to be the last chamber. There was indeed a glass bottle hanging from the ceiling, but I couldn't see anything or anyone inside it.

Half a dozen boys turned to look at me. Slaves held torches aloft. The boys' faces were kohled and rouged, so they seemed halfway between boy and girl. When they saw us they all prostrated themselves.

I looked at Petronius.

To my astonishment ... dismay, even ... they were grovelling in front of *me*, not my master.

And they cried out in chorus, "Ave, Augusta!"

'What do you mean?" I said. "I'm not an Augusta."

"I knew it," said Gaius Petronius Arbiter. "You have a destiny higher than the house of Petronius."

"But they are calling me Empress," I said.

"Are you displeased?"

"Bewildered," I said. "I'm a boy."

"That," said my patronus, "is in the hands of the gods."

"But isn't the Sybil going to say anything?"

"She speaks all the time," said Petronius, indicating the song of the cricket. "The boys translate."

"So can I ask what they mean?"

The boys rose from their prostration. One who seemed to be their leader spoke to me. He said, "You who shall be Empress …" and the others said, "Ave!" Then he said, "You who shall a second time be Empress," and the others said, again, "Ave!" And finally, he said, "You who shall reject the title of Goddess …" and the others again hailed me.

It made no sense, and the incense assailed my nostrils and I could barely breathe.

"No prophecy for my master, who brought me all this way?" I gasped.

The boys did not prostrate themselves to my patronus. Instead, their leader said, "You are wedded to death, but you shall not die." Another boy said, "Your hands will bleed ink." A third said, "Your bastard will be your truth."

"Oh, why can't oracles tell you anything real?" said Petronius. "Come, my Giton, was this not worth an entire gold piece?'

"It's a hoax," I said. "There isn't even anything *in* the bottle."

"Probably not," he said, shaking his head.

We turned to leave, but the way out was blocked by centurions, and at their head stood Tigellinus, Nero's right-hand man, commander of the Praetorians. I'd even been to his house before. He was, I am sure, the one who had agitated for Petronius's removal. He stood there in the smoke, smirking.

"Am I under arrest?" said my patron.

"Not exactly," said Tigellinus.

"I see," Petronius said, "I'm to be slaughtered right here, in a sacred place, while praying to the gods?"

"You don't even believe in the gods," Tigellinus said.

"Who would?" said my master. "Seeing what they have wrought in this world?"

"I tend to agree," Tigellinus said. "But, you're a nobleman, and we're civilized people. The usual conditions will apply, of course; you commit suicide properly, formally and with honor, and the state doesn't seize all your assets."

"Why, there's nothing of mine you want, Tigellinus? Not even a pretty vase, a valuable old manuscript, or the odd villa?"

"Not really," said Tigellinus.

"You never did have any taste."

I could see the Praetorian visibly restrain himself from striking my patronus. It was a peculiar game these aristocrats played, cloaking their hypocrisy behind lip service to some archaic code. I was surprised to see Tigellinus following the code; I had supposed him a simple brute.

"We will escort you back to Rome," Tigellinus said, "so that you can set your affairs in order and take care of this, ah, matter. Can we supply a physician? Himself the Divinitas could provide his personal doctor, an expert in making things painless."

"No need, Tigellinus. I'd rather not travel with an escort. It's not a good look," said Petronius. "People might talk. Rest assured, this … *matter* you allude to … will be taken care of correctly and expeditiously."

"It's better if we accompany you."

"Don't you trust me?"

Tigellinus sighed. "I suppose I do, really." He waved, and let us through. Just like that.

I tried to pull my master by the hand, but he insisted on walking slowly, in a dignified way. "Hurry, domine!" I whispered. 'What a stroke of luck! You could be on a ship by morning."

"On a ship? You think I mean to escape, like a slave?"

"I only thought —"

"Oh, my innocent Giton! Where would I go?" said Petronius. "Rome is my life."

XXX

AVE ATQUE VALE

Petronius's last symposium had to be perfect in every detail. And Croesus and the household slaves made it so. There were only a few guests, and all of them poets, his rivals, even; none of them would have wanted to miss the evening. There was a magistrate, too, and an official clerk. And Marcus Vinicius as well, his nephew.

It was difficult because the slaves were all weeping as they served the cena. Hylas was the sole delicatus and served the wine daintily, somehow clenching back his tears.

Before dinner, Petronius had already had a physician open up a vein, but then he had it bound up again, so that he would be able to enjoy the company of his friends.

Despite the fact that Rome had only recently burned, the culina managed a reasonable spread. No larks' tongues or fattened dormice, but the calves' brains in honey were sweet and succulent, and the homely dishes like roasted pork were well seasoned, and there was a good quantity of Falernian wine, which is the only wine that is strong enough to burn.

My former master read aloud some passages from the *Satyricon.* Then he grew bored, and asked instead to hear the classics. And so I quoted Sappho to him:

Come to me now
Release me from my harsh distress,
from all that my heart yet longs for…

"Ah," he said softly. "An ode to Aphrodite." He was weakening, but he smiled at my choice of poetry. "You have come so far in so little time," he said.

Presently he ordered the entire household to gather in the triclinium. And I was to learn why there was a magistrate present, for that night, Gaius Petronius Arbiter officially made known his last will and testament.

"As to the disposition of my inheritance," he said. "It shall be thus. Please, clerk, make a note of all I say, and magistrate, have everything entered officially, so that no questions can arise later. First, let my estates outside Rome become the property of my nephew, Marcus Vinicius. Let him take possession of my slaves, except for the ones I shall name herewith, who shall be manumitted upon my death. And this the little apartment attached to this villa, and all the furnishings therein, fall to my steward, Croesus, to whom I now award his freedom." He named a few more slaves to be freed, some immediately, some whom he asked Vinicius to free "after a certain period of time, as he deems fit." And he continued for a time in this vein, dispensing also a few perfunctory whippings to some of his more ill-behaved slaves, which were carried out on the spot. "And I bestow the delicatus named Hylas to my freedman, Gaius Petronius Gaii Libertus Sporus."

Hylas gasped, and he threw himself at my feet. He began kissing my toes, which I thought a little undignified.

I did not know what to think. I could not imagine myself owning him. He was really a friend, not a piece of property.

"Me do everything you ask, domine," he said to me. I found his abjectness disturbing. Perhaps I should simply free him in the morning.

"Don't be sad, Hylas," Petronius said. "I could free you, but what would you do? I don't want you working in a lupanar, you're far too delicate for such abuse."

"Me not sad, domine. Me happy to belong to Sporus."

I raised Hylas to his feet. "Be happy," I said.

"Don't beat me too much," Hylas said, and kissed me on the cheek. So, I kissed him on the lips, and the guests applauded.

"Pour yourself some wine, too, Hylas," said Petronius.

"Domine ... no, me not presume."

But in the end, we did get Hylas a little drunk, and he began babbling in his own language, an odd guttural-sounding argot, and he was doing a strange dance which he said came from his village. And the guests even laughed a little, almost forgetting the solemnity of the occasion.

Then there was more small talk. Nothing about the Emperor. Nothing about the fact that my patronus was slowly bleeding to death, carefully attended by his physician so he could remain conscious enough to entertain his guests until the last minute.

Finally, Gaius Petronius Arbiter called me over to sit with him. "I want to feel you close to me one last time," he said, "since we are bound for different worlds, me to wander Avernus as a lost shade, you to inhabit Olympus as a goddess … I will not see you even in the next world."

"Patronus," I said, "even if that were true, I would use my powers as a goddess to summon you to me."

"So sweet of you," said Petronius, and kissed me on my brow. "But now, I want you to do me two favors," he said. "My final commands to you, so please do as I ask."

"Of course, patronus," I said.

He beckoned to Croesus. Slaves brought the wine dipper to him. It was a beautiful object, made of some purplish crystalline material, carved out of a single large semi-precious stone. I had seen it only at Petronius's most exclusive parties … now that I thought about it, only at the very first symposium I had arrived at, the one where I hadn't been wily enough to talk my way out of a lashing.

"Do you see this? It's the most precious object in my house — apart from you, that is, and even for you I paid less. This was three hundred thousand sesterces. Now, pick it up… and … over there, do you see that marble column? Fling it as hard as you can, and make sure it's quite thoroughly smashed. I'd do it myself, my darling Giton, but I'm bleeding to death, as you know."

I knew it must be something that Himself coveted, so I did as I was told. I'm just a weak boy, trained in pleasure, not soldiering, but I did a creditable job. It broke in several pieces and would never be repaired. Perhaps it was because I threw it with all the rage and disillusion I was feeling, and all the terror that this whole world that had formed itself around me when I came to Rome was now crashing down around me. The wine dipper was smashed in any case, and the guests applauded.

Then Petronius had a scroll brought to me. He sealed it

several times. And he said, "Tomorrow, Sporus, you will give this letter to Nero."

He did not say to the Divinitas, or any of the many circumlocutions we always use. "Before you ask," he said, "it's a catalogue of every infamy, and every scandal, and every hurtful thing he has ever done. It is my last word to him as his Arbiter of Elegance."

"But I can't deliver that — he'll kill me!" I said, panicking.

"You are the only person the Emperor *won't* kill for delivering this message."

This I could not believe. Yet, it seemed to me that if Petronius was going to leave us, there was not really any meaningful existence for me, either. By tomorrow, it would all be over.

It was then that the home of Petronius Arbiter was visited by no less a person than the Empress herself. She had come in secret, with only a small retinue. She stood in the doorway of the triclinium and a hush fell. What was there to say?

She stood there, elegantly and simply dressed in an imperial purple stola bordered with gold thread. Her face was whited with lead pigment, so she resembled one of the statues of the gods.

"Thank you for coming," Petronius said softly.

"I wouldn't miss it for the world," she said.

"You're not here to gloat, then," he said.

"Hardly," she said. "You've been a shining light in our artistic chaos. And you were instrumental in causing me to attain my goal. I assure you, this is not my choice. But it's the Praetorians who rule in Rome … not the Divinitates."

"Yes, Divinitas," said Petronius.

"No hard feelings, then."

"Of course not. It's just politics," said my patronus.

This was the Roman upper class. It was not proper for them to be concerned with death. Properly brought up nobles were ready to take their own lives at a moment's notice, and not make a fuss about it. It was just politics.

Poppaea Sabina walked up to where I was sitting, and she put her hand on my shoulder. "Tomorrow," she said, "I'll send an escort for you."

"And when you return from the palace," said Petronius, "you will also take possession of this house."

"Domine!" I cried out, though I was sure I would not live to inherit the house, for surely Nero would find a way to seize it.

"I will make sure of it," said the Lady Poppaea Sabina, the mistress of the world, whose every fold of flesh I was intimately acquainted with, who had the power of life and death over me. "You can trust me, Sporus."

She took my hands and I looked up at her face.

Could I really trust her? I had to, at least for now.

I saw a hardness there that I had not seen before. Having such power must have seeped into her soul. But I saw something else, too, something I had not expected to see.

What was I to her? Wasn't I just a plaything, a boy who chanced to resemble her so closely she could use me as a pawn in her little games of power?

But now I saw that in addition to all that … she also feared me.

XXXI

AMOR ET MORS

When the symposium was over, a few of us carried Petronius to his cubiculum. They laid him gently down and said their farewells. Petronius told me to remain. "It may be more dignified to let me die in peace, but I want the last thing I see to be beautiful."

He sat me down beside him and the physician knelt down and loosened the bindings so the blood could once more flow freely from his wrists, running into a priceless antique red-figure vase from the days of the Athenian Republic.

When everyone had left, I gazed down and saw that his eyes held an exquisite serenity.

"You didn't finish the *Satyricon*," I said.

"Life is full of unfinished things," he said softly. "You, my Giton, are unfinished, too."

"Everything I am, you made," I said.

"And would that I could have made more. But you are to be Augusta, and perhaps a Goddess in your own right, as well. Oh, I wish I could see the spectacle. Sporus, you are the ideal, the perfect boy, the perfect woman." But his tone, as always, held irony.

"I am neither, and I am not perfect," I said.

"*Mundus vult decipi, ergo decipiatur.* Translate into Greek," he said, sounding as cranky as Aristarchos when I wouldn't apply myself..

"The world wants to be deceived, so let it be deceived," I said.

"I won't be an empress," I said, "I won't be a god. I'll let myself be burned along with your funeral pyre."

"Don't be a silly boy," he said. *"Cito fit, quod dii volunt."*

He said no more to me, but I stripped down to my subligaculum and lay down beside him, and held him, heedless of the blood that spurted all over me. I murmured many words to him, foolish words of a thoughtless child, perhaps, how much I loved him, how much I hated him for leaving me. I babbled. He was silent.

I didn't think I could fall asleep, but weariness overcame me in the end.

And so I awoke at dawn, blood caking on my arms and legs, and Gaius Petronius Arbiter was gone. Someone had come in, closed his eyes, perhaps, and covered him with a woolen blanket; they had left me sleeping.

I shifted, carefully climbed out of the bed and made my way to the bath. Hylas was already there. "Salve, domine," he said to me.

"Don't call me that," I said.

"Sorry, domine," he said. He untied my subligaculum and followed me down into the hot water, and started to scrub away the dried blood.

"There, you clean now," he said.

"But I don't feel clean," I said. I didn't think the blood would ever wash off.

After I had soaked for a time … though I felt no less dirty … Hylas scraped me off with a strigil and oiled me. I smelled of roses. But I still felt unclean on the outside, and empty on the inside.

Hylas dressed me in a plain tunica and cloak fastened with a bronze fibula. "Now you are beautiful dominus," he said softly.

When I left the bath I could see that Petronius's body had already been bathed, anointed with perfumes, dressed in a clean toga, and that he was laid out on a low bier in the foyer. Behind him was the atrium. From the other walls, the death masks of ancestors looked on. A little incense burned on the altar of the lares and penates. Hylas led me in and I saw the household already gathered.

The libitinarius was already there, taking detailed notes from Croesus about the funeral arrangements. The slaves were weeping, some quite noisily. When I entered they looked at me with a strange kind of apprehension and awe. Gradually, they fell silent. I did not weep. I only felt the emptiness.

I was, I suppose, the master of this house, though I felt nothing at this, just the same numbness. The notion of being a dominus made no sense. All I knew was that my world had ended and I knew no other; I could not even return to my village, for I did not even know the name of the country it was in.

Presently there came Petronius's clients … all wealthy people had such hangers-on … I noted that the poets who had been so eager to attend the dinner-party last night were absent … and all of them went directly to Croesus, who knew each one by name and was able to say something appropriate, such as "Yes, the master thought of you often," or "The master wished your son to have such-and-such a trinket" and so on.

It was clear to me that all this had been planned for a very long time, probably long before any word had come about charges of treason. Croesus worked with a preternatural coolness and efficiency. He was surely the finest steward money could buy. He was free, too, now. I wondered whether he, too, felt empty.

Croesus invited me to sit on a curule behind the bier, for all the world like the young heir of the estate. Marcus took a stool beside me, but in a secondary position, as though I were the main inheritor of his uncle's fortune.

"Did he say anything to you before he died?" he asked me.

"Only … that when the Gods want something, it happens quickly," I said, for those had been his last words to me.

"True enough," said Marcus grimly. He, too, did not weep, for that would have been unseemly for a patrician whose relative had done something honorable by taking his own life.

I sat like a stone for the rest of the morning, not eating or drinking though wine and refreshments came around many times.

Around the fifth hour, someone came for me from the palace. A small company, in fact, led by a centurion. I took Petronius's letter and followed the soldier to the waiting litter. As I stepped out onto the street, I vomited.

Hylas rushed after me to wipe it off. I went back inside for a change of clothes.

This time I was steadier.

"Are you quite all right?" said the centurion.

"I'll be fine, now," I said.

"Me go with you, domine," Hylas said.

"The boy stays behind," said the soldier. Hylas tried to follow regardless, but the centurion gave such a threatening look, I was sure he was going to strike him. Disconsolate, the boy turned back and reentered the house. The other slaves watched me, all with expressionless eyes, afraid.

I was sure I would never see any of them again.

I closed the curtain of the litter and did not look outside until we reached the Palatine.

And yet you did see them all again. Indeed, you survived, and will continue to survive until ...

The climax of these games? My apotheosis? I wonder. Why aren't I dead already?

The program has been switched around a little bit. It seems that your throne is still being gilded, and the performer playing the role of Hades had an unexpected ... mishap.

The God of Death met an early death?

He had a big match this morning against a wiry little Gaul. The audience didn't like his attitude, so he got a big thumbs down. He's normally very popular. I think he was just getting into character to play your rapist, so he acted a lot more arrogant than usual. They call him the Black Elephant; he came from far to the south, beyond Egypt, and the size of his member was a marvel; the Gaul tossed it to the crowd, so you won't get to experience it up close, I'm afraid. They're searching for a suitably magnificent replacement. They'll want to see your impalement right up in the plebeian seats.

They really want me to die spectacularly —

As you lived, Divinitas. So now, they're flooding the arena now for a sea-battle, and your death-scene will come after that. Once they've found a Hades of the right dimensions.

Oh. Flooding the arena. That explains the smell. The tang of the ocean wind is in the air.

They'll move you to another cell, on higher ground, soon. This level will get too damp. Perhaps, while they ready your next ... royal chamber ... you'd like to go and watch them preparing the sea-battle?

So I can get a bit of fresh air before I'm deified?

Yes, Divinity.

Shall we go?

Careful with the narrow steps. I haven't worked all day on your makeup to get it all smudged.

Oh yes. They've brought in real sea-water. But there's not much wind. It's stagnant. Perhaps they'll find some way to whip up the waves.

No expense is being spared.

The story of my life ... and of my death.

But we've arrived at quite a turning point. You are on your way to see Himself, with the catalogue of his depravities, penned by the world's greatest satirist, in your hands. What do you say to him? And how does it happen that you are not crucified on the spot for such insolence?

Later, my friend. A breeze has sprung up. For now, let me enjoy the wet fragrance of this artificial ocean, and reflect on how my journey began, with chains and the sea ... just as it will soon end.

Let me smell the salt and the breeze for one last time; then I'll tell you about what it was like to be mistress of the world.

Thank you so much for taking this journey with me into the story of Sporus, one of the most extraordinary figures in ancient history.

There is much more to the story, and what becomes of Sporus after he has visited the palace with Petronius' message, and how he became first Nero's Empress, then survived the reigns of Galba and Otho only to be sentenced to die in the arena while playing the role of the goddess Persephone.

If you feel like it, please leave a review for the book if you purchased it on amazon. The link can be found here:

https://www.amazon.com/Delicatus-S-P-Somtow-ebook/dp/ B0BR88V6VZ

If you can't wait to go on with the story, and have access to a U.S. Amazon account, check out the Vella section where the second book is being serialized.

Printed in Great Britain
by Amazon

33589239R00139